ANITA: A TROPHY WIFE

Sujatha (1935–2008) was one of the most popular authors in Tamil literature and his literary career spanned more than four decades. Widely-read and knowledgeable, his versatility and exhaustive range were his unique selling points.

Writing in simple and lucid Tamil, Sujatha made a tremendous impact with his contemporary and racy writing, and his radical and original ideas. His experiments with different genres, and the dramatic narration of ordinary, everyday events won him his audience and many accolades. His works stood out at a time when Tamil writing was dominated by social and family dramas and historical novels. His identification with the masses, and his depiction of their way of talking, behaviour, mindset, dialect and slang, helped make him popular across multiple demographic segments.

* * *

Meera Ravishankar is a lawyer, an educationist, a language and communication trainer in addition to being a writer and translator. Meera loves taking on challenges, and is happy to straddle many worlds, be it writing text books for school children, training corporates, developing content or doing translations.

Meera has done bilingual translations both from Tamil to English and English to Tamil. Her notable translations into Tamil are Chetan Bhagat's *Two States*, *Revolution 2020*, *Five Point Someone* and Rujuta Diwekar's *Don't Lose Out, Work Out!*

An ardent fan of Sujata and his writings, Meera is grateful for the opportunity to introduce Sujatha to a larger audience.

ANITA:
A TROPHY WIFE

SUJATHA

TRANSLATED BY
MEERA RAVISHANKAR

Published by
Rupa Publications India Pvt. Ltd 2023
7/16, Ansari Road, Daryaganj
New Delhi 110002

Sales centres:
Bengaluru Chennai
Hyderabad Jaipur Kathmandu
Kolkata Mumbai Prayagraj

Copyright © Sujatha 2017

This is a work of fiction. Names, characters, places and incidents are either the product of the author's imagination or are used fictitiously and any resemblance to any actual person, living or dead, events or locales is entirely coincidental.

All rights reserved.
No part of this publication may be reproduced, transmitted or stored in a retrieval system, in any form or by any means, electronic, mechanical, photocopying, recording or otherwise, without the prior permission of the publisher.

P-ISBN: 978-93-5702-676-5
E-ISBN: 978-93-5702-638-3

First published in Tamil in 1971
First published in English by Westland Publications Ltd
in association with Mysticswrite 2017
Published in English by Rupa Publications India Pvt. Ltd
in association with Mysticswrite Pvt Ltd 2023

First impression 2023

10 9 8 7 6 5 4 3 2 1

The moral right of the author has been asserted.

Printed in India
This book is sold subject to the condition that it shall not, by way of trade or otherwise, be lent, resold, hired out or otherwise circulated, without the publisher's prior consent, in any form of binding or cover other than that in which it is published.

SUJATHA: *Writer nonpareil*

SUJATHA (1935–2008) was the pseudonym of the Tamil author S. Rangarajan. He was one of the most popular authors in Tamil literature and his Tamil literary career spanned more than four decades. Widely read and knowledgeable, he presented his knowledge in simple and lucid Tamil. Most of his writing was intended for the commercial media, but never did he compromise on the quality of his work.

He worked in many fields, was a bibliophile and hence was inspired to write in a whole range of genres and on a number of subjects. As an engineer with BEL, he invented the voting machine. He also worked in an airline. His versatility and exhaustive range are his unique selling points. Actor Kamal Hassan once commented that 'for the biggest love of his life, Tamil writing, Sujatha baptized it with his lady love's name' (Sujatha was his wife's name).

Sujatha's writing style was his biggest contribution to the Tamil language. It was full of energy, innovative, minimalistic and often mischievous. His columns for Tamil weeklies such as *Ananda Vikadan, Kumudam* and *Kalki* were widely read and won him numerous fans across all age groups. He drew thousands of youngsters to Tamil literature with his lucid and engaging style. Among his famous writings was a column in *Kanaiyazhi (Kadaisi Pakkam)*, which was known for its brutal frankness and rapier-sharp comments. In fact, for this column, he wrote in his original name and even criticized his own works penned in the name of Sujatha!

His style is also acclaimed as natural, incidental and never contrived. Despite his vast vocabulary he is known for his sharp writing, never waxing eloquent and significantly, never attempting an 'overkill'. He did not exaggerate events or emotions, remained rooted to reality but at the same time never trivialized. His humour was often self-deprecating. He also visualized the scene and painted the picture vividly for the audience. He believed that, just as in films where twenty lines of meandering writing can be condensed into a single frame, one's writing style needed to be tight and gripping.

He was the first to write science fiction in Tamil. He made science easy and accessible to the layman. He even compiled a list of Tamil-equivalent words for computer terminology.

He began writing in 1962 and never stopped—making an impact with his trendy and racy writing, his radical and original ideas, experimenting in different genres and creating a dramatic narration of ordinary, everyday events which won him his audience and many accolades. His works stood out at a time when Tamil writing was dominated by social and family dramas and historical novels. His identification with the masses, and his uncanny adoption of their way of talking, behaviour, mindset, dialect and slang, helped make him popular across multiple demographic segments.

Often accused of being overly influenced by Western

ideas, he once clarified that they were recreated to fit into the Tamil arena. Many tried to follow his inimitable style only to fail because his writing was subtle and never explicit and loud. He made Tamil engaging and colloquial—a great flow, at times hilarious and often brilliant—never boring! His choice of vocabulary was not only apt but picture perfect; his technique, descriptions, emotions and edge-of the seat, thriller-inspired, flashy narrative style are well known. He also had a penchant for depicting the absurdities of life.

Sujatha's strength was that he wrote of things that he knew. He often used contexts and settings that he knew in real-life in his novels and they would invariably revolve around the following locales: Srirangam, Chennai, Bengaluru, and Delhi. He was a clever storyteller: characters and environment are brought to life with brilliant observation, and then penetrated deeply with sharp satire.

Most people who met him in person emerged dazed by his warmth, his hospitality, his willingness to learn and exceptional humility. He used to jocularly comment: 'Never visit your favourite writer; for the scales may fall from your eyes!' But he was an exception to this.

Among his favourite writers was P. G. Wodehouse, who died while typing a word on his typewriter; Sujatha said he would also like to write until his last breath, which he did!

One of his pet phrases was: 'It isn't *kamba sootram*'; meaning, nothing is rocket science. He had the supreme ability to break concepts into 'byte-sized' inputs and also make them interesting and relatable! One could say he enhanced the reader's quality of reading and walked companionably along with them in their journey of exploration and intellectual discovery.

Among others, Sujatha immortalized the characters of Ganesh–Vasanth—an imaginary advocate pair serving as the main characters in most of his detective stories. Ganesh is a level-headed, senior advocate and Vasanth is his flirtatious junior. The Ganesh–Vasanth pair was probably based on James Hadley Chase's characters, Vic Malloy and his sidekick. Vasanth is a character through whom he documented the changes that he observed happening around him. Vasanth keeps changing his car, the style, the lingo, and his women!

Anita—A Trophy Wife (Ilam Manaivi) brings out the nuances of a power struggle in a very distinctive style. This is his second book in the Ganesh–Vasanth series, though Vasanth did not make an appearance in this novel. The book describes the strained relationship between a middle-aged man and a beautiful young woman in poignant and simple terms. It is a story that happens again and again. In Sujatha's deft telling, this story acquires a timeless dimension.

MEERA RAVISHANKAR

FOREWORD

The first-ever serial I wrote was *Nylon Kayiru* for the Tamil weekly *Kumudham*. *Anita-Ilam Manaivi* is my second. I suppose I wrote it in 1971. I had simply called it Anita. The editorial board at *Kumudham* changed it to *Anita-Ilam Manaivi*. They might have thought that this title would titillate readers and create more interest in it.

Meanwhile, my novella *Gayatri* was published in *Dinamani* magazine. Film director Panchu Arunachalam wanted to make a movie on it and asked for its rights. At about the same time Anita was also being serialized in *Kumudham*. Panchu Arunachalam, who happened to read Anita, desired to make a movie on it too. When *Gayatri* hit the theatres, another movie was simultaneously making waves: Bharathi Raja's *Pathinaru Vayathinile*, which created an impact in the industry and set a new trend in Tamil cinema. Rajinikanth's punch dialogue, *Idhu eppadi irukku?* (How is it?), became a much-repeated catch phrase.

Panchu Arunachalam is a sentimental man. On getting the filming rights for *Anita*, he decided to release it as *Idhu Eppadi Irukku?* It had an impressive star cast, including Major Sundarrajan and Jaishankar. But the movie itself was a disaster. The way it was made, no title would have made a difference. But Panchu Arunachalam was not one to give up. He next made *Priya*. I was personally not thrilled by the manner in which it was picturized, but then, it had other aspects like Singapore, the dolphin show, Ilayaraja's classic melodies—all of which contributed to its success. Later, of course, Arunachalam gave up on my novels.

SUJATHA

BEFORE WE BEGIN...

The girl, perhaps eighteen, had the special teen bloom, look and image. Her eyes showed a little alarm; they also displayed a wee bit of interest. What was the fear and interest about? The guy was taking her along with him. It was a lonely path. One could see the military radio centre's tall aerial masts at a distance. Blue sky. Rocky area. Slopes, wild flowers, yellow blossoms. She knew why he was taking her. Both sought isolation. Both were in the prime of their youth. They had been intimately acquainted. The closeness of their relationship had given them the courage to explore further intimacies. However, that had not been sufficient. They craved even more. And this burning desire made them cross some boundaries they had earlier set in their relationship. After crossing some forbidden boundaries, they came here with plans to breach more barriers and explore further frontiers.

Before going any further...

His name: Anand. Her name: Radhika. Place: Delhi; Month: November; Time: 3.30 PM

They kept walking. There was a slope to the left, patches of green grass and flowering trees all around: Jacaranda, Gulmohar, and other colourful shrubs vying to create the ambience of a park. His eyes searched for something in particular. The place was not crowded. That's why they had chosen it.

Let's eavesdrop on their conversation:

'Look, what a beautiful flower!' She remarked.

'Oh, yes. It's quite pretty,' he agreed.

'Radhika…'

'Mmmm…'

'Come with me.'

'Why?' (All pointless questions … meaningless answers. She was walking with him and she also knew why.)

'Did you ask why? I want to share a secret.'

'What secret?'

'Let's go.'

'Where?'

'Come with me. There are people around here.'

'Do you need to be alone to share a secret? Why don't you say it right here?'

'It's not a secret that is meant to be told.'

'Then…?'

'Is this a new necklace?'

'Don't touch me on that pretext.'

'Just checking if it is new….Ah! Why would you pinch me?'

'You don't keep your hands to yourself.'

'Honey, sugar, darling…'

'You always seem to—Where are you going?'

'Are you coming or not?'

'I'll come only if you tell me where.'

'You see, it's a flower; a pretty one at that; very pretty. It's in a tough, inaccessible place. I need to approach it slowly, very slowly. I need to pluck it without causing pain.'

Her blood warmed and she flushed.

'Let me stay put here.'

'Look, I cannot pluck it without your help. I need you badly. Please come.'

They approached a large concrete wall with a water pool behind it. An artificial brook flowed by; and circular concrete slabs were laid across it. The ground had a natural rise and slope leading to shrubs, bushes, grassy plains and trees; trees...and more trees behind trees; a dense patch of trees, dark and isolated; a lonely, verdant darkness.

'That's a good place,' he said.

They reached there. He scanned the place. A few birds were twittering. 'No one can see us,' he said.

They heard a distant rustle. A man wearing white pants was crossing the patch. He appeared as a white flash through the foliage.

'Not here' she baulked.

'Let's walk some more,' he suggested.

They walked further.

The ground suddenly dipped in to a deep, beautiful and intimate crater. He leaped into it with ease. He waited for her to follow him. She hesitantly jumped in. He held her tight and put her down gently and slowly.

She shrieked in excitement. Then placed a hand on her breasts to calm herself, and then looked around.

'None can see us,' she reassured herself.

The green grass at their feet was invitingly soft, like a bed. He plucked a blade of grass and started chewing on it. 'How is this place?' he asked.

She slowly surveyed the landscape.

A mud path from somewhere snaked towards them. 'I see a path,' she said.

'No one will come this way,' he said cockily.

'Are you sure?'

'Have you ever come here before?'

'Oh no!'

He moved closer and sat right beside her. 'Is this a new necklace?'

'Seriously, are you enamoured by my necklace? Let me take it off for you.'

'No. I don't want it at all.'

'No...no...no...!'

'Yes...yes...yes...'

'Hey! Wait, please. I beg of you, please...'

He hugged her hard. His right hand splayed across her back possessively.

He was so close to her that he could observe the exact shade of her lipstick and possibly write a whole treatise on it. He leaned towards her.

She suddenly let out a piercing scream. It was one of stark terror. 'Look there...Look! Look!' She could barely whisper.

There was a body in the direction she pointed. Supine on the green grass. Facing the blue sky. The eyes certainly looked dead; mouth gaping open; one leg folded and bent at an odd angle; the other stretched out. The hands looked numb and the fingers had frozen in the position when the body had been alive...rigor mortis had set in, and now it was most certainly a dead body!

ONE

'Click!'

The camera blinked once. Soon after, the photographer walked around to choose another angle to click; he adjusted the view-finder to focus on the image carefully and...'Click!'

Inspector Rajesh lit a cigarette. He drew in the smoke deeply with relish. He paused. He exhaled the smoke with pleasure. He looked down. The person on the ground was about fifty years old. The Terylene shirt he was wearing was one size too large for him. He wore new shoes. He had bruises on his forehead and neck. Constables were intently searching behind the bushes. Anand was standing in a corner. He borrowed a matchbox from the inspector and pulled out a cigarette from his own pocket. Before lighting it, he said, 'Inspector sir, I have a request.'

Without even looking at him and in a distracted manner, the inspector said, 'Hmm...?'

'Can I leave?' Anand asked.

'No,' replied the inspector shortly.

'You have asked me all the questions, right?'

'There are a few left. Why did you come here, a place which is inaccessible to most people?'

'Just like that.'

'Hmmm,' the inspector remarked. 'Try another lie.'

'It's not a lie.'

'Where's that girl?'

'Girl?!'

'Your girl?!. You must have sloppily removed the lipstick stain from your shirt earlier. Just before the police arrived...'

Anand looked down at his shirt, and then at the inspector, who also appeared young. He smiled and said, 'Yes.'

'Where is she?'

'Why do you need her? I found the body. I reported it. I've given my address. There's no need to involve her.'

'You should not hide anything from the police. Don't you know?'

'Inspector Saheb, I came here, I saw the body and reported right away. I could have slunk away quietly. No one would have come here for days on end. I did my duty and feel that I have not failed in performing it.'

'That's true, thank you.'

'So can I go?'

'Wait. We need a statement from you. What's happening?' The last was addressed to a constable.

'Sir, we found a car.'

'Where?'

The inspector thought to himself... 'This is going to be easy...' The constable accompanied the inspector along the snaking mud path for about a furlong. The path led to the main road. Right at that intersection they found a lone car that was abandoned on the incline. No one could have noticed it from the main road. It was parked at an angle so as to remain hidden from the road. One of its doors was open.

'Don't touch it,' the inspector warned the constable.

The car looked new and was totally undamaged, but it was dusty. The keys weren't in it.

The inspector instructed the constable, 'You wait right here,' and walked back towards the body. The constable guarding the body was waiting for him. The photographer was seated on the grassy floor. 'Sir, we found this on the ground,' said the constable, and handed over a key case. Inspector Rajesh opened it. It had the car key, petrol tank key and another key.

The inspector touched the body for the first time. He felt revulsion while touching it. On searching the pockets, he found a wallet. He opened it and found it to be empty. Riffling through it, he found a visiting card in one of the compartments. The card had elegant gold embossing. 'R. K. Sharma, Neelima, 47, Vasant Vihar, 616645' was printed on it. It was only then that the inspector had a closer look at the bruises. He thought: 'This is surely not a natural death....When could he have died? The wallet and car keys have been found. Thankfully the name and address are there. The car keys are there. Double check.... How could he have died? He is so cold. They will now take him to the mortuary, conduct his autopsy and submit a report. They will measure the wounds in the neck. The report will carry numbers and metrics and descriptions of all his wounds and his bruises would be listed out.... They will dissect the stomach and cut out a small tissue.

The tissue will be immersed in chemicals in a test tube in the lab. The teeth will be closely inspected. They will not overlook the gash on his head with the blood caked dry.

Sharma! R. K. Sharma. Vasant Vihar. Big shot for sure...'

'Inspector, may I leave?'

(This guy is such a bother! But he's ok. One needs immense courage to report. Anyone else would have evaded and escaped.)

'Come to the station, and then you can leave. Mr. Narayan...'

The photographer approached.

'Please hang around for a while; 3850 and 715 are here too. Let me make a call and arrange for the body to be carted to Wellington.'

'Could you get me a 'paan' on your way back?' requested the photographer.

'La la la la...!'

The smell of sandalwood permeated the air; warm water was gushing from the shower, and the tiles were gleaming white. She slowly turned around so that the water could embrace her in its warm comfort. She was in a pleasant daze and continued singing. The water droplets slid along the curves of her body, straightened, then meandered, then paused before they trickled and dropped down.

The telephone had been ringing long and hard in the bedroom. Thinking she heard something, she closed the shower to hear it better. There...she could hear the telephone pealing. Yes! No doubt. The telephone *was* ringing. She didn't rush out. Slowly grabbing a spotless white towel, she dabbed herself gently. The mirror facing her reflected her naked image up to her breasts. She quickly wrapped the towel around herself. She slipped her feet into flip-flops and softly opened the door. She started walking, completely ignoring the many wet parts of her body. The bedroom had a telephone extension, which rang relentlessly. A Pekinese dog which matched the white of her towel was waiting eagerly outside the bathroom door. The moment she emerged, it wagged its tail briskly and followed her with glee.

'You are also going to have your bath today,' she promised the dog and picked up the phone.

'Hello!'

'Is it six-one-double-six-four-five?'

'Yes.'

'What is your car number?'

'Who is this?'

'Police.'

'What is it about?'

'What is the number of your car?'

'Which one? We have two.'

The water from the wet places had slowly trickled and formed a puddle at her feet.

'The Fiat.'

'TLK 2520. Why are you asking? Has there been an accident?'

'Who is on the line?'

'Mrs. Sharma.'

'Mrs. Sharma, please come to the Wellington hospital immediately. It's an urgent and important matter.'

'What is it? Why don't you tell me now?'

'Did your husband leave home in that car?'

'Yes. He has gone to some place in Haryana. He left yesterday. He said he would be back tom—'

'Mrs. Sharma, I'm sorry to interrupt. I am forced to say this. The car was found abandoned in a mud path forking from Upper Ridge road. About a furlong away, in a dense, isolated bush, we found a body. We presume it could be your husband's.'

'What do you mean by "body"? What exactly?'

'A dead body.'

'O God! God!'

'Mrs. Sharma, we are sorry that not only have we delivered this grievous news insensitively over the phone, we are forced to inconvenience you further. You need to come to the Wellington hospital and identify the body. Or you could send one of your acquaintances…'

'I shall come myself. It can't be him. I hope it is not him.'

'We shall send a jeep to your house shortly and—'

She hung up like an automaton.

TWO

Bhaskar, Sharma's personal secretary, played for the king of diamonds. He did not get it.

Then he tried for the queen. No luck.

Knight or Jack, as they call it…hmmm…no way…

The moment ten was dropped, he threw an ace in and took the whole hand. What a great card player Bhaskar was! He seemed to predict and read his friends' cards like a mirror reflection. He knew his partner would not have any diamonds in his suit.

Bhaskar started playing his spades. The third time he dropped his queen, the knight and ten landed. He got nine lots as if he had counted each of them out personally. He held on to three—no trump—and dropped the rest of the cards.

Bhaskar was known for this quality: excelling in his task and finishing it to perfection, a silent worker.

When Bhaskar was stacking the cards for the next game, he heard a car honking at his door.

The short honk conveyed immediacy and urgency. A short blare from a distinctive horn, it was his boss's big Mercedes horn.

Bhaskar excused himself from his friends and leaned out of his balcony.

The petrified driver was waiting outside. The moment he saw Bhaskar, he said, 'Please come down immediately.'

Bhaskar pulled a shirt on, pushed his feet into his sandals and slid down the stairs. He was still buttoning his shirt when he came near the car.

'What?'

'The boss is dead!'

'What? How? Where?'

'Get into the car and I'll brief you. Madam is waiting in the hospital.'

As Bhaskar jumped into the Mercedes, it came alive at the snap of the driver's fingers and vroomed away, like an arrow shot out of a bow.

Hospital

Inspector Rajesh lifted the white cloth from the body's face.

Anita took a hasty look. 'Please, I beg of you, please close it.' She put her head down.

'O my god! So many bruises!'

'Mrs. Sharma, this body,...'

'It is my husband.' Saying this, she moved away to a corner, covered her face with the *pallu* of her sari, and started sobbing.

The white cloth covered Sharma's face again.

Bhaskar entered. He also identified it as the body of his boss.

Anita went back to the car. She got in. Her cheeks were flushed red. They were swollen. Her face and head were partly hidden by her sari. She placed a thoughtful finger between her eyebrows, bent her head and patiently waited to leave.

Inspector Rajesh and Bhaskar were standing near Anita's car. The car was humming in neutral gear and Bhaskar instructed the driver, 'Go straight home.' He then looked at Anita and said, 'I have asked Meenakshi to come. I will also call the Doctor saheb. You please rest. I shall join you in an hour. The rest of the things will be waiting for you at home.'

Anita did not respond. She didn't lift her face. The car moved. Its red tail lights blinked angrily once and then seemed to simmer.

'She is very upset,' said Bhaskar to the inspector.

'She is young,' commented Rajesh.

'Inspector sir, just the day before my boss left for his trip, he withdrew a lot of money. Mrs. Sharma might know exactly how much.'

'Where did he go?'

'Hissar. He has a factory there.'

'Did he leave alone?'

'No. Govind went along with him in the car.'

'Govind! Who is that?'

'His man-servant.'

'Where is Govind?'

'Where is he indeed?'

Time: Two days after the meeting at the mortuary
47, Vasant Vihar

On the way to Palam airport, a new wealthy colony had sprung up—Vasant Vihar. Young architects had gone crazy with their imaginations and each house reflected this. If one were to stand here and take a good look around, one would refuse to believe that India was a poor nation.

When Inspector Rajesh reached Sharma's residence at number 47, he had exactly this thought. Such a palatial mansion for just two or three people!

It was a two-storeyed house. A modern first floor; concrete squares, green creepers, an outhouse. There were smaller houses at a distance, probably servants' quarters; two garages and a concrete extended porch that acted as a temporary car park. The house was completely covered with glass windows—double glass panes. Brick red screens, tasteful modern furniture for guests to lounge in the living room, a centre table with magazines strewn on it.

Rajesh announced his arrival to a servant and started browsing the magazines.

In one of the pages of the magazines', a signature had been practised many times—Anita, Anita, Anita. *'Alright Anita, I mean Anita Sharma....How old would she be,'* thought Rajesh. Maybe twenty-eight years old. He had met her for the first time under these unexpected tragic circumstances at the hospital. Her husband was dead and she was grieving; even in such a grave situation her beauty, her physical beauty, could not be hidden, and it seemed to disturb the hospital staff. Eyes and looks fell on her and all were arrested by her beauty and distracted by the lure of her spell. Doctors seemed to wipe their spectacles to take a good look at her. Anita...

'Good morning, Inspector!' Bhaskar disturbed his reverie.

'Good morning, Mr. Bhaskar. How is Mrs. Sharma?'

'Better. Did you get any information on Govind?'

'No. We have telegraphed the description that you provided to all the states. Our ASP is taking a personal interest in this case. He will come this afternoon. He has asked me to conduct some preliminary interrogation and investigation.'

'Shoot away.'

'I need to interrogate Mrs. Sharma.'

'I haven't seen her yet. She has locked herself on the first floor. She hasn't eaten at all. This incident has upset her a lot. I shall ask someone to check on her. Ram!'

Ram entered. Bhaskar instructed Ram to fetch Meenakshi. When she came in, Bhaskar pulled a notepad out of his pocket, scribbled a note and told Meenakshi, 'Give this to madam.' She left.

'Who is this girl?' asked Rajesh.

'Mrs. Sharma's aide. A poor girl—the boss's distant relative.'

'Mr. Bhaskar, I need more information about Govind. What was his nature of work here?'

'He was like a valet, helping the boss in his personal matters. He used to constantly hang around with Mr. Sharma, give him massages, polish his shoes, and lay out his clothes.'

'How long has he been employed here?'

'It's about eight years since I joined. He was around even earlier. I have heard that he has been with Mr. Sharma since his childhood.'

'Where did he stay?'

'Right here...in the outhouse.'

'I would like to search the outhouse.'

'Sure.'

'There's another issue.' The inspector looked at his notes, licked a finger and thumbed the pages. 'Oh, yes! The money...you said Sharma withdrew a lot of money and probably carried it with him. Can you prove it?'

'I had gone to the bank the previous day and withdrawn fourteen thousand rupees. I am not sure how much of it he carried with him.'

'Why did he go on the trip? He could have sent you.'

'There was a problem, a delicate issue in the factory. He left to resolve it personally. Also, I was on leave that day. I had taken some guests to Agra for sight-seeing. Otherwise, under normal circumstances, I would have accompanied him.'

The inspector wondered in which context Bhaskar had used the word 'accompanied'. Nevertheless, he proceeded with his enquiry. 'Mr. Bhaskar, is Govind capable of murdering his boss for fourteen thousand rupees? What sort of a person is he? I would like to hear your opinion of Govind, off the record, of course.'

'It's a trifle tough to answer this question. I feel it's difficult for me to classify people as murderers or not. But...'

'But?'

'These are the facts. Govind went with him in the car. Sharma has been murdered. Govind is missing. If we connect the dots, two plus two would be...'

'Before we decide it is four, there are plenty of questions that arise. Sharma left for Hissar on the 18th night. The body was discovered on the 20th evening. Doctors place the time of murder to be the early hours of 20th morning. So, what did Sharma do on all of the 19th? Where was he?'

'I called the factory at Hissar. They said he never visited.'

'I also cross-checked that information. We need to account for one whole day now.'

'How did he die?'

'He has been beaten, kicked, stamped on and strangled to death. Surely two or three people must have been involved.'

Meenakshi entered and gave a note to Bhaskar. Right under Bhaskar's note was scrawled: 'Ask him to come.' Bhaskar showed the note to the inspector.

Anita wore a simple white sari and white blouse. She was devoid of make-up. She wore no bindi. Her hair was dishevelled. A plate containing food lay untouched next to her bed.

Even after the inspector entered the room, she showed no signs of talking. She was silent. Bhaskar dragged a chair close to her. The inspector sat on the edge of the chair and faced her.

Anita hesitantly started, 'Bhaskar...' Her voice was as soft as a malleable, thin golden strand, so fragile that it might break with a touch. It sounded like a baby's whisper.

'Yes?' replied Bhaskar.

'Moni? Has she been informed?'

'I have sent her a cable yesterday, Mrs. Sharma.'

'Who is Moni?' asked Inspector Rajesh.

'His daughter, only daughter...She is studying in America,' said Anita.

'His daughter, eh? You have a...'

'I am his second wife,' said Anita.

The inspector did not know how to react. Silence prevailed for a while.

'Mrs. Sharma, I just have one important question. Does your husband have any professional enemies in business? Are there any heirs fighting for his wealth? Who is the beneficiary of his death?'

'I do not know.'

'Mr. Bhaskar, would you know?'

'I have some sketchy details. All of his wealth is self-acquired. There are no issues or disputes over it. He has written a will. I know of it. I brought the advocate home. But I do not know the provisions of the will.'

'There shouldn't be any difficulty in gathering that information. Doesn't he have any son?'

'No.'

Anita said, 'He treated me with affection. He loved me deeply. Inspector, he was a good man. He did not bear ill-will for anyone. Why did he have to face such a cruel fate?

So many wounds, bruises! Oh dear mother!' Anita's eyes closed. She leaned her head back and kept still. Her eyes glistened with unshed tears. The only noise was from the fan which was whirring pathetically overhead. Her sari fluttered. Meenakshi stepped closer, hugged Anita and set her sari right.

'Bhaskar, please come with me,' said the Inspector.

As soon as they came to the ground floor, Inspector Rajesh was dying for a smoke. He asked for Bhaskar's permission, opened his pack and offered one to Bhaskar, who said: 'I don't smoke.'

Rajesh picked one for himself, tapped it on the box, placed it between his lips, lit it and took a long indulgent drag. Only after the smoke filled his lungs did his frayed nerves calm down and his excitement recede.

The outhouse was in the backyard. It was tiny. Only one person could stay in it. The door was open. The rooms were open too. There was a kitchen to the left, followed by a miniscule bathroom and toilet. There was a garden behind the house.

'This is where Govind stayed,' said Bhaskar.

There was just one built in cupboard. An Indian Oil Corporation calendar hung on the wall. The cupboard had a picture of Lord Vishnu. A packet of incense sticks, dried flowers, a faded mirror and a steel trunk in the last shelf were total contents of the cupboard.

The inspector opened the trunk. White khadi shirts

folded and arranged neatly, two khaki pants, a notebook, a few Hindi novels and a pen were found inside.

'Hmmm,' said the inspector.

'What are you looking for?'

'I need Govind's photograph. Can I get one?'

'Photo...photo...' Bhaskar thought aloud. 'Let me try. His photograph may be in the family album.'

'Was Govind a bachelor?'

'Yes.'

'How old would he be?'

'Forty, forty-five years.'

'What is his home town?'

'I think he hails from Uttar Pradesh. But he has stayed for many years with the family. His dad had worked for this family too. At that time Sharma's family stayed in Patel Nagar. They were not so wealthy or influential. Sharma was an extremely hardworking businessman. Luck also favoured him. He had a Midas touch. He transformed everything to gold. This house has been built recently; it's just two years old. This is his dream house—his Taj Mahal!'

'Built for his first wife or the second?'

'OK! You want to know more about Mrs. Anita Sharma?'

'Yes.'

'I do not know the details of where he met her. He married her two-and-a-half years ago. He was completely enthralled by her. One cannot merely tag it as love, affection or fondness. I must say it was an obsession.'

'She is a beautiful woman.'

'Yes.' Bhaskar took a keen interest in his fingernails. He avoided meeting the inspector's gaze.

'One more thing…did Govind carry any weapon?' asked Rajesh.

'I don't understand.'

'You might find this question strange. Have you ever seen Govind using a whip?'

'A whip?'

'Yes, a whip. Look here Mr. Bhaskar, we found that Mr. Sharma's body was covered with whip-lash wounds, cuts and bruises…'

'Oh, no!'

THREE

Lawyer Ganesh was angry. There were a quite a few reasons for his anger....

The cleaning woman had not turned up for the day; Mulla's *Hindu Law* was steeped in dust; the errand boy had served him tepid tea which looked and tasted like dish water! Ganesh was intent on completing a brief, but no matter how much he shook and rattled his pen, it neither budged nor wrote. Goodness! A series of catastrophes that led him to seriously consider plunging into matrimony; it seemed like a haven—mere child's play compared to his present stress levels.

'Mohan ! Mohan, you little devil! Where the heck are you?' Ganesh screamed at the top of his voice.

The door opened.

'You silly fool, what is this? Is this your idea of tea? God forbid that your grandpa—God! I am so sorry!' He froze in mid-curse.

The person who entered was not Mohan at all. It was a young wisp of a girl.

'I'm dreadfully sorry! I was hollering at my servant! Please be seated! Ah! Please don't sit. Let me dust the seat for you.'

'You have a novel way of welcoming people,' she remarked. Barely twenty-two, she had cut her hair brutally short and coloured it brown. With every step of hers, her hair moved too. She was wearing some bling made of beads around her neck. The circular pendant resembled an antique coin. Her face had the vestige of a child, but she wasn't smiling. She looked anxious. Her cheeks looked flushed, but certainly not because of make-up! She appeared as though she had been rudely thrust into the folds of a tropical climate from a colder region and the sudden change in temperature had left its red marks on her cheeks. She wouldn't smile; not at all. So there were no hints about the shape and form of her teeth. She had thin lips. She reminded one of a fragile glass piece that would crumble at someone's touch. Her arms did not match her height and looked uncommonly thin. Her sari was simple and could not be accused of any dressiness. She wasn't all that thin, but it would help if she gained a few pounds. She had big, all-consuming eyes. They were now gazing at Ganesh.

'I'm Miss Monika Sharma.'

'Pleased to meet you, Miss Sharma! I'm Ganesh.'

The ease with which she shook hands suggested that she must have a distinct western influence. At the same time, the handshake was limp. So he presumed that she was upset or scared.

She took a seat and he too sat down.

'Five days ago, my father died,' she said.

'Oh! Is it that Mr. Sharma? I'm so sorry. I did read in the paper that he had been murdered and that his missing servant could be a suspect...'

'Yeah!'
'Has the servant been found?'
'No.'
'I'm sure they will find him,' said Ganesh.
'I haven't come to discuss the servant.'
'I know.'
'I need your help.'
'Ask away, and I shall help. But I charge by the hour.'
'My dad...'
'Sorry for the interruption. Who sent you to me?'
'Vijayakumar.'
'R. N. V.?'
'Yes.'
'Isn't he in America?'
'I'm from there too. I'm studying in America. On being informed of my dad's death I landed in India yesterday.'
'Is that so? Now I understand.'
'What?'
'The reason for your handshake...'
'It is bad etiquette in India, huh?'
'Not at all...tell me.'
'Would you happen to know the actual details of my father's murder?'
'I just skimmed through the paper and don't believe newspaper accounts. So you can fill me in.'
'The night of the 18th, my dad took his man-servant Govind along in his car to Hissar. He has a factory there. I'm told he was carrying fourteen thousand rupees. My dad never reached Hissar. On the 20th evening, his body was

discovered lying near a bush in a park past Upper Ridge Road. No trace of the money, and Govind is missing too.'

'Please continue,' Ganesh gently encouraged.

'I received the cable way too late. I did not have ready cash. I finally garnered the money, and then had to beg and plead with Air India for a ticket. By the time I landed here, four days had elapsed. My dad had been hurriedly cremated and I didn't even get to see his face. My only living memory of him is the image I carry in my mind when I left two years ago.'

The girl was under deliberation and tried to control the onslaught of tears that threatened to spill. Her eyes mirrored her discomfiture. She tried to wipe her eyes surreptitiously with the edge of her sari. She must have forgotten her handkerchief.

'I can feel your grief. Words cannot assuage the loss, I'm sure. It may take days, months, even years....Shall I get you some tea?' asked Ganesh.

'No thank you.'

'Something cold, then?'

'No thanks, Mr. Dinesh.'

'Ganesh.'

'My mother died when I was way too young. Since my seventh year, I have been housed in convent hostels. While my dad was busy chasing money I was crying to myself, seeking comfort by hugging a pillow, thinking of my mother and pining for her in tiny hostel rooms. All the other girls would receive snacks and short eats from home regularly. They would get fond letters. All I would get is money mailed by my dad's secretary. Very rarely would dad's car arrive. When he did visit, it would only be for a minute. He would flood me with presents—chocolates, frocks—and rush back to the nearest airport without even waving good-bye. I have never stayed at home. In fact I don't even remember having one. Much later, he built a house, a wonderful one at that. He took me there for a visit and said: 'This is our house; our dog; our servants; our car. This is Anita.' That's how he introduced her to me.'

'Anita?'

'Yes, Anita—the last milestone in my dad's endless path of success. She's just six years older than me. My dad's trophy wife! You must see her to believe her. She's ravishing, to say the least. How did she come to be his wife? I do not know. Why did she come? Why did she agree to marry my dad? It's a mystery. I have no answer. As effortlessly as he would step into his garden, pluck a favourite flower and pin it on his coat lapel, he acquired his trophy wife too. The only house that I got in my entire life had become Anita's. Her beauty and smartness reflected and echoed in every nook and cranny of that house. Do we need to make soup today? Ask Anita. Should the dog take a bath? Ask Anita. All of them became Anita's slaves. She had my dad on a very short leash in her bedroom. At his age he lusted after her so much!'

'You articulate things well.'

'Look Ganesh. You needn't patronize me. I'm seeking friendship desperately. I bet I'm much younger than you. So I need, not your respect, but friendship.'

'Right. Let's start on equal terms and on first-name basis. Let's be friends.'

'Agreed.'

'Agreed. Go ahead and complete the rest of your story.'

'I did not appreciate the way Anita used my dad. I seemed to be a stumbling block for their second honeymoon phase. I made great efforts to stay out of their way. Luckily, I received a scholarship from America. My dad gladly got me a first class ticket in a Boeing and packed me off....Now he could spend his time exclusively with Anita without me as a hanger-on. They must have been relieved as they were running out of excuses to send me away to movies or the Gymkhana club or to play tennis. I spent two lonely years on alien soil. In all that time I would have received a total of about two or three letters. Those were also: 'Anita wants a Sony tape recorder; she would like a Sharp television; don't forget to buy them for her.' I've never had a dad all my life and eventually what a death he has faced! Today Anita is a widow. She cries copiously and her tears look real to me. At times, I even feel pity for her. At other times, I regret that more than half of my dad's holdings will have to be shared with her. This is the end of my tale.'

'You said you need my help, right?'

'Yeah, I seem to have forgotten all about that. Aren't you a lawyer?'

'Yes.'

'My dad has made a will. According to that I get the rest of the property after handing over Anita's share to her. I read the will. Bhaskar showed it to me.'

'Bhaskar?'
'My dad's secretary. A good fellow.'
'Hmmm.'
'I don't understand head or tail of the will. The sentences are too long and convoluted. I feel that there is some complexity in it. I would like you to check it out. You can pore through it, analyze it and then let me know the following details: What would my share be? How soon can I claim my share? Should I pay tax? In which office should I get it processed? Whom should I smile at to get the job done? I need your advice.'

Ganesh smiled. 'I'll take care of everything. It is enough if you just smile at me. Why don't you smile for me now?'

She gave him a slow smile. For a split second their eyes met, clashed and then averted. She moved away.

'That's better. Now I have some questions. Do you have your dad's death certificate?'

'I do not know. Bhaskar might.'
'We need a death certificate for sure. How old are you?'
'Twenty-one. Should it be proved?'
'Yes. We need to establish that you are not a minor.'
'I have a driving licence. I used to drive in Wisconsin.'
'Do you have your S.S.L.C. certificate?'
'I need to search for it.'
'What do you plan to do with your share of the money?'
'Spend it.'
'I must examine the will,' said Ganesh.
'Why don't you come home? Vasant Vihar. A beautiful Pekinese dog named Shoba is around. My very beautiful

stepmother lives there. Her name is Anita. She is such a phenomenal beauty that you would have never clapped your eyes on a woman more beautiful.'

'I understand that you don't really like Anita.'

'*Wah re wah!* My dear Sherlock's son!'

He felt she was a smart and bubbly girl, so casual and easy to talk to. *At her young age she seems to have developed a deep psychological insight into human nature and has developed a sharp, smart and functional sixth sense. She will definitely come up in life by herself. She is capable of taking care of herself*...were Ganesh's thoughts.

'What are you looking at?' asked Monika.

'You are OK,' he said.

'Why do you say that?'

'You will survive. No one can cheat you. Also, I am around, so don't worry.'

'I'm sure that's not what you were thinking. You must be like, "After all, her dad's dead for hardly five days and this girl is already calculating her share of the money! She must be a strange character!" Wasn't this your thought process?'

'No, not at all.'

'Even if you did think on those lines, I don't give a jot. Let me repeat myself. I have no dad. My mom is in my memory as just three letters...m-o-m! My dad was a machine—one that kept spinning money in excess, later fell in love, surrendered and became a completely defunct machine. I cannot cry over a machine. I have cried so much that all my tears dried up by the time I turned fifteen.'

'No tears; what about Coca-Cola?'

'Come, let's go out and grab a bite. This room stinks like a printing press.'

'Wait, let me get my car.'

'You don't have to flaunt your car. Let's just take a walk.'

Ganesh locked his house and joined her. She was already on the road waiting for him. He realized he wouldn't be able to go to court that day. He needed to get an adjournment. He decided to call his junior Sunil Kumar from the hotel.

'So, Ganesh, I don't have any money on me now.'

'I do.'

'Start an account in my name. Keep tabbing all that you spend for me. As soon as I get my dad's money I shall settle your account.'

'Will do.'

'Do-re-mi-fa-so-la-ti...' she sang.

'Silly girl!'

'Why are you walking away from me? Are you shy?'

'Out of respect...'

'My foot!'

'Monika, at least considering the rest of the world you need to stay demure for a few days.'

'I shall follow my lawyer's advice.'

Ganesh was waiting in the Sharmas' living room. Monika leaped up the stairs, two at a time.

Ganesh looked around.

The living room reeked of money: paintings, screens, silk, enamel, mosaic, plastic, silver mirrors, wall-to-wall carpets, the green lawn outside, the water fountain, a Satish Gujral painting, an air-conditioner, a television. Now, had he missed anything?

'Ganesh!' Monika bent from the first floor and called out. Ganesh looked up. He noticed the lingerie visible through her neckline.

'Come up!' she ordered.

Ganesh climbed the stairs slowly. He checked his hair. 'Do you need a comb?' she asked. 'No,' he replied.

They entered that room together.

Is that Anita? She must be for sure, Ganesh thought, just a wee bit hesitant. He restrained his crazy urge to let out a piercing wolf whistle. What a woman!

FOUR

Anita was wearing a sea-blue sari; she was just standing, but it seemed like she was radiating a special halo of light. The sari *pallu* barely reached her shoulder. It was a short sari. She wore just traces of compact powder. Lips, eyes, nose, the solitaires gleaming in her ears, a flood of dense midnight hair, flashes of a slender neck, her curves, her breasts, hips, feet, toes, fingers, eyelids, eyebrows…Is there even a single blemish anywhere?

'Anita…this is Ganesh. Ganesh, meet Anita and Bhaskar.'

'Pleased to meet you,' said Bhaskar.

'Who is this?' asked Anita.

'My lawyer,' answered Monika. 'Bhaskar, please show dad's will to him.'

Bhaskar looked at Anita, as if seeking her permission to do the bidding.

'Just a minute. There is no rush. Let me introduce myself properly. I'm Ganesh, as you already know. I have come to scrutinize the late Mr. Sharma's will, after which I need to clarify and explain the provisions to Miss Sharma here.'

'He is my lawyer. Doesn't he resemble Mastrogiovanni, the football player?' she gushed.

'Moni!' warned Anita.

'Yes, my dear co-respondent. Isn't that the right legal term?'

'Moni, your dad has just died and you are so...'
'I never had a father, Anita!'
Anita kept quiet. Her face had streaks of worry lines. Ganesh anxiously intervened. 'Monika, I would like to talk to them in private. If you are around, the conversation cannot happen. So please...'
'I shall return in half an hour. Anita, I'm taking your car out, I mean mine,' said Monika.
'Bhaskar, can you leave us alone too?' suggested Anita.
The window curtains billowing in the breeze seemed to reflect Ganesh's restless mind.
Anita sat down. She looked at him and held his gaze unwaveringly. 'How long have you known Monika?' she asked.
'For the past thirty minutes.'
'Did Monika talk about me?'
'Yes. All that she said is true!'
'What did she say?'
'Anita—isn't that your name? She said that you are ravishing!'
'Tch!' she was vexed. 'What do you think of Monika?'
'She is a baby. The rage of her slighted youth is unbridled and is shooting in all directions.'
'She hates me. She believes that I am somehow responsible for her dad's death and that I'm connected with it in one way or the other...'
'She did not say so to me.'
'She would have said that I married him for money, that I am a gold digger.'

'She didn't say that either. She is lonely. She seeks affection. She has never experienced genuine affection so far and misses it.'

'True.'

'She desires a home, not a physical structure. A place to get back to in the evenings, a place steeped with childhood memories. She never had that, which is the cause for her anger and indignation. She has no roots for her memories. She doesn't hate you.'

'No. I do know that she hates me for a particular reason. When she was just about to get closer to her dad I intruded. So…'

'Quite possible.'

'How old are you, Mr. Ganesh?'

'Thirty-two.'

'Married? Children?'

'Neither.'

'Why?'

'Haven't established myself in my profession yet.'

'What would be your guess about my age?'

'Twenty-eight. Monika has already briefed me.'

'Twenty-nine.'

'You don't look it.'

'I have become a widow at twenty-nine. What have I gained out of life? You talked about Moni's loneliness. Let me tell you about mine. Sharma bought me for a price. He met me, fell for me. He acquired me. Just like that—he picked me off a shop window like he was purchasing a shirt. A trophy wife!'

'Is that so?'

'Everyone thinks I married him for his money. Today, right now, you can create a document for me. I shall sign it. Let it all go to Monika. This house, Patel Nagar house, Clark's hotel, shops, company shares, gold, diamonds—everything, all of it can go to her. Please inform this to her. She doesn't know of Anita's depth of character.'

'I don't know what to say. In a span of a mere two hours, my mind is crowded with plenty of contradictory narratives and details.'

'Please tell her this too. I have suffered enough at her dad's hands after marrying him—his jealousy, his suspicion, lust and more have plagued me and troubled me.'

'Really, Mrs. Sharma, I think this conversation is taking us to exceedingly intimate and personal issues.'

'You can call me Anita now. I have been liberated from the tag of Sharma. He had me in a gilded cage, fed me apple crumbs and readied me for his bed. I have escaped from the hands of my lustful tyrant. I don't need even a penny from his wealth. I'm an educated woman. I can get a job. I can take care of myself. You are a lawyer. Please do me this favour. Get the documents ready. Release me and free me from the clutches of this house.'

'I feel both of you need to cool off. Only then can we reach an agreement.'

'My anger will not cool down in this birth.'

'Mrs. Sharma, let me just ask you one question. Why was your husband murdered?'

'The money that he chased constantly has killed him.

He has been killed for a paltry sum of fourteen thousand. His servant killed him.'

'Is there no other reason?'

'No. Why? Do you think there could be some other reason?'

'Not really.'

'Then why did you even ask?'

'Just thought of it, so I asked. Forget it. I understand your problem and its gravity completely. Your life is not done. Do not throw away the money that has come your way just because of momentary anger clouding your mind. Look at it as a compensation for all the exploitations you have faced all along. Don't make hasty decisions.'

Anita remained silent. She gazed out of the window.

Ganesh seized the opportunity to take a good look at her. He tried to visualize her in various roles—the queen of a house, in an old man's bedroom, as a village belle, as a waif on a railway platform, as a princess, as a movie star, a diva, a young widow...

Young widow? No way! Right in front of me is Anita in a blue sari with her voluptuous body; she can't be a widow! I'm thirty-two and she's twenty-nine, he thought. Ganesh now imagined her standing close to him. Right next to him... She appeared all decked-up and resplendent with her bindi shining and smiling at him. He imagined her walking closer, approaching him, and...

'What are you thinking?' asked Anita.

'Nothing.'

'Would you like some tea?'

'No, thank you.'

He found Anita's door to be ajar; he took a quick peek to ensure that no one was around...

As he couldn't restrain himself, he blurted out: 'Really! I can't imagine you being an old man's wife.'

'Shall I tell you the reason for marrying him?'

'If you like...'

'You won't believe me.'

'I'll try.'

'When I was eighteen, I was also living in a dreamy, fanciful world. I wanted to study medicine but couldn't. My dad was just an ordinary clerk. He made a lot of efforts to educate me. I studied B.A. Home Science. I wanted to help my dad financially. So I scouted around for a job. I got one in Delhi. I became a civilian clerk in the Air Force station. I am not proud to admit I got the job based on my looks. I was aware of it. I was not comfortable at my workplace. Right from the corporal to the wing commander, all of them lusted after me. I'm basically a shy person, quiet and reticent. I could not handle all that attention and quit the job. The only good thing was the friendship I had developed with Flight Lieutenant Raja. Raja was my Prince Charming. I don't think I shall ever meet another man like him in my life again. He was such an affectionate, humane and polite man. He chatted with me, laughed with me. He completely overwhelmed and possessed me. He wrote letters, narrated anecdotes and kept me thoroughly engaged. As ill luck would have it, he was transferred to Agra. But that did not deter him. He asked me to move to Agra and marry him right away. But my dad was sick at that time and I had to attend on him. Raja promised he would return after a week to meet me. He never did. He died in an air crash!'

Ganesh listened to her story quietly.

After a while, she asked, 'Have you read Omar Khayyam?'

'I have read parts of it.'

'I can never forget these lines of Khayyam:

I sometimes think that never blooms so red
The Rose as where some buried Caesar bled

My Caesar Raja bloomed a glorious red in the battlefield of my mind after his death!'

'What happened after that?'

'I did not feel like getting married after his death. I worked as a typist and a receptionist. At every place of work, my beauty became an issue, so I had to quit. I then took up a job where they paid three hundred rupees per hour to play hostess in a hotel. I smiled at him just as I smiled at everyone else. He was Sharma, the hotel's owner. I became the Cinderella discovered by an aging prince. I could not handle the tornado of his courting. He sent flowers. He showered me with silk saris, movie tickets and gifts galore. He called me into his room and implored with tears in his eyes…Practically begged me, saying that all he needed was my loving care. He assured me that marrying him would not restrict me in any way. He went to the extent of saying: 'I shall give it to you in writing. Why don't you just give it a shot? If you don't like me you can be free the next minute!' On those false promises, on those false words—words that shone like gold and pearls—I agreed. And that's it! The tale of my life took an ugly twist after that.'

She was quiet for a few moments, then continued: 'I was locked in a cage. Night, day, mid-afternoon, evening—he desired me at any time of the day, at all times of the day. He needed me constantly. Another man dare not look at me and I mustn't look at anyone else. God forbid, if I did, there would be plenty of questions! By making false vows and pretexts, he had tricked me into his possession. I could never venture out of the house alone. Meenakshi would always accompany me. I had to eat on time, sleep on time, and watch movies only with him. He was so worried that someone else would occupy the seat next to mine in a theatre that he would reserve the entire row. Not a speck of dust was allowed to settle on me without his permission. If I just so much as snivelled, a doctor would be summoned. Of course, it goes without saying that it would be a lady doctor. If I went to take a bath, he would be waiting outside to shelter me from the world's eyes with a towel. I needed to be around him 24/7. If he happened to travel on business, I had to be locked up in an air-conditioned room and never step out till he arrived. It was a strange kind of a torture by smothering! Mr. Ganesh, do you think I need his money? Tell me, after this entire torture, do I need it at all?'

'He was a strange man indeed.'

'He wasn't human.'

Ganesh suddenly recollected what Monika had told him.

'She is holding my father on a short leash in her bedroom.' Now who had chained whom?

'My life should have had a different course. But I have landed here, you see,' said Anita.

'It's not all over and done, Mrs. Sh...Anita.'

'It's definitely done. But when was it done? I feel it was that fateful evening when my Raja died in Agra, the evening that I received the news of his death. My dad was sick, lying in his room. I opened the door. A gentleman in Air Force uniform was standing outside. 'Are you Anita?' he asked. I said 'Yes.' He said, 'Flight Lieutenant Raja asked me to give this to you. He was travelling by a transport plane. It met with an accident. He was grievously injured. In his last hour of pain he was calling out your name. He wrote a letter and asked me to hand it over to you.' He gave me a stainless steel chain which Raja had worn. Raja had managed to scrawl three words: 'Anita, don't forget!' Can I forget? Please tell me. Is it ever possible for me to forget?'

Anita began sobbing uncontrollably and tried sitting down, but collapsed.

Ganesh did not know what to do. A bachelor all his life, he was feeling inept in a situation he had never faced so far. How does one console a crying woman? Ganesh went near her and bent down.

'What is this, Anita? You are not a child. You should not break down like this.'

'They are all accusing me of being a gold digger, hankering after his wealth. Isn't it enough that I have undergone much personal shame? Isn't all this enough?'

'No one is accusing you. You seem to be imagining it all. Please get up.'

She refused to get up. She slid further down on the floor. A stainless steel chain was visible around her neck. Her clothes were dishevelled. Had she fainted?

The streak of tears from her eyes trailed up to her ear. Her beautiful lips had parted. The white of her teeth and the pink of her gums were visible. She sighed so hard that Ganesh was worried that her blouse would burst open.

Ganesh lifted her and carried her. Just as he was about to lay her on the bed, Monika entered. 'What happened? Have I interrupted anything?' she asked.

'Shut up! Anita has fainted.'

'Really! Bhaskar! Bhaskar!'

'Monika, please open that window. Get some cold water from the fridge.'

She called out to Meenakshi, who asked what had happened.

'Get some cold water. Madam has fainted. Quick!' said Monika, adding, 'Ganesh, why don't you try artificial respiration?'

Ganesh hated Monika for the first time.

Bhaskar rushed into the room with great urgency. He noticed Anita was lying on the bed. He glared at Ganesh. He called the doctor immediately on the phone. Meenakshi came in, stroked Anita and comforted her.

Ganesh stepped out of the room. Monika accompanied him. Ganesh descended the stairs quietly. Which woman should he believe? Which one was lying? Tough...truly tough. No woman was lying completely, but then they weren't speaking the complete truth either. 'They are mixing up truth and lies, the percentage of the mix being uniquely different. Do not believe any of it entirely,' was his advice to himself.

FIVE

Anita's subtle compact powder lingered on Ganesh. She was light like a feather and he had found it effortless to carry her. A comfortable weight indeed!

'What did you ask, Monika?'

'Are you going to stay here till she recovers or are you leaving?'

'I will leave.'

'On whose side are you now?'

'Both of you are on the same side...which is the unanimous hatred for your father.'

'What did Anita ask about me?'

'What did Moni ask about me...? That was her question to me. Both of you are intent on biting and chewing the other's head off. I shall study the will later.'

'Wait! Let me ask Bhaskar to show it to you right away.'

'Not now, Monika. I need to go to court. I will definitely come later.'

'Now this tells me that you have changed your mind about me.'

'I haven't formed any impressions yet.'

'Let me drop you.'

Once in the car, her focus was on the road and she spoke with nonchalance, 'Ganesh, I need your help. I approached you first. So do not forget that.'

'Anita, don't forget!' was the note left behind by Raja. Ganesh recollected that now.

'Monika, have you read Omar Khayyam?'

'No.'

'Anita has read him.'

'Don't tell me! Did she speak of Omar Khayyam all along?'

'She shared some details about herself. She clarified why she married your father.'

'What was the reason? Pure love, eh?'

'No point talking to people who are so cynical.'

'I don't need Anita's self-account or history. She is an extremely attractive woman, I agree. Grief knows no shame—on that tenet she seems to be exposing a lot of her body. Your roving eyes devoured all of it. She is a bitch!'

Ganesh was astounded by the word Monika chose to describe Anita. A woman using such a word was strange! Ganesh said: 'Look, you can think what you want about her. In my opinion, most of what you think about Anita is wrong. Your hatred has affected and clouded your perspective. I'm not worried about that. But don't use such foul words from now on. It's neither fair nor cultured.'

'She has lured you well—you have fallen into her trap and you are besotted with her like the rest.'

'Stop the car. I need to get down.'

'Come on, lover boy! Don't get annoyed over such trivia—'

'Are you going to stop or not?'

'I won't.'

Ganesh switched off the ignition and grabbed the keys. The engine sputtered and the car came to a grinding halt. He opened the door and got down. He threw the keys in and walked away.

She trailed him in the car slowly. 'Ganesh, I'm sorry,' she said.

'Don't need your sorry...Check the sari that you are wearing...Taxi!'

Ganesh wrote in his diary that night:

Monika, 21 [mental age 14]; Anita, 29, what an awesome person! In a matter of two hours, so many autobiographical accounts. How was the old man? Must meet the inspector. There's something missing, something wrong with that family, and it is circumstantial....With whom? Where? A tiny bird was tweeting that something is certainly wrong.

He was contemplating what else to write. His telephone rang. He wrote something and scored it out. 'Ganesh,' he answered the call.

'Ganesh! Is it Ganesh? Anita here. Please come right away, please. Won't you come over, please?' She sounded anxious and alarmed.

'What happened, Mrs. Sharma?'

'Someone is attempting to murder me,' she replied.

When Ganesh reached the house, he found Anita sitting on a stool in the portico. She appeared dishevelled and shattered.

'What happened to you, Anita?'

The white dog was barking next to her. There were no other people around. Monika had gone for a movie. Bhaskar had gone home. Ganesh noticed that there was no watchman at the gate.

Anita's neck had a red weal. There was no blood, but finger imprints had left angry red marks. She could barely speak. 'I will not…I cannot get into that house. Ganesh, please take me away. I will stay in some hotel. I don't want to step into that house.'

'What happened? Why don't you tell me?'

She breathed hard. Her words slurred. 'There's no one at home. I sent Meenakshi away. I was reading. The window opened a crack. I thought it was the wind. I turned around a little distracted. It…it…was…he…He was standing there!'

'Who?'

'Someone…he walked straight towards me. I was paralyzed for a few seconds. I couldn't run immediately. Meanwhile he ran towards me, put his arms around my shoulders and pressed me down. I pushed him away and bit him.'

She was quiet for some time. Her bangles were broken and had grazed her arms. She continued with her tale: 'I made a tremendous effort to get away. My clothes got torn. He chased me across the stairwell. I screamed 'Help! Help!' I rolled over the steps, fell down the stairs…He…he…didn't follow me down the stairs. I almost fainted. I gained consciousness some time later. The moment I realized my plight, I called you. I've been sitting outside, waiting for you.'

'Anita, did you happen to look at his face?'

'I couldn't see clearly. It could be my fancy. He reminded me of Govind.'

'Govind?'

'As I said, it could be an illusion. Ganesh, I don't need this house or the wealth. I only need peace.'

'It's wrong for you to be alone. Don't stay alone from now on. You need to be treated for your bruises. Come, let's go in.'

She protested.

'Another thing, Anita. Did he attempt to kill you or did he touch...?' he asked.

'I'm not sure,' she said. She turned around and he saw that her blouse was torn.

'Come, let's go in.'

'Where?'

'To your room.'

'I don't want to.'

'Ok. Let me go in then.' He climbed the stairs.

She called out, 'I will also join you. I am scared to stay alone here.'

A stool had rolled over on the first floor. A glass tumbler lay broken. A pearl string had snapped and the pearls were strewn all around. He switched on all the lights. He searched. He looked out of the open window. He pulled the screens.

It was dark outside. In the distance, he could see Palam airport; a flight was getting ready to land, its tail-lights blinking red. The green lights on the wing tips seemed to answer the red by blinking back. Total darkness. Who had come? He turned around. Anita was inspecting the scratches on her arms. 'Where is the medicine cabinet?' he asked. She pointed. He reached inside it and took a wad of cotton. He also took out the bottle of Savlon. He sat her down and dabbed the Savlon-soaked cotton on her wounds to clean them. What a piteous woman she was! Head bent down, she was making great efforts to curtail her sobs. One caring word, and she would break down, and the tears would start like the opening of flood gates, beware! Ganesh decided he dare not say anything commiserating.

'Do you firmly believe in the possibility that it might be Govind?'

'No, I am not so sure. I thought it just may be him. That's it. In my fear and anxiety, I did not notice properly.'

'Why did he go away?'

'My dog was barking vociferously. That could be a reason.'

Ganesh went near the window again. Something rustled in the darkness. What could it be? Or who? Was it an illusion, his mind's projection? What could he do about it?

'When will Monika return?'

'She didn't inform me. I do not know.'

'It's better you have Meenakshi around for at least a few days.'

'No! I am quitting this house right now, today!'

'You have no place to go now. I shall wait till Monika comes. Did you have anything to eat?'

'No. Did you?'

'I've had dinner.'

'I'm not hungry.'

She was scared, he thought.

'Why don't you sit down?' she suggested.

He sat down. 'You need to change your clothes,' he observed.

'I'm scared to go into that room.'

He did not reply. They looked at each other. The look contained the question, the answer and the explanations.

'Ganesh, close that door.'

He closed the windows.

'Not those, the room door.'

'Ganesh, switch off the lights. All of them.'

He complied.

When Monika arrived later, Ganesh was in the living room reading a magazine.

'Surprise! What brings you here?'

'How long do I have to wait for you? Which movie was it?'

'Some silly movie...Never mind. Did you come here in search of me?'

'Yes.'

'Where is Anita?' asked Monika.

'I did not see her. When I came she was seated here. I asked her for you. She said that you were out and asked me to wait. She was quite brusque and went away after that. Is she unwell?'

'Who knows? You aren't annoyed with me any longer?'

'I was never angry with you.'

'Is that why you jumped out of the car?'

Ganesh refused to honour that question with an answer. He seemed to be harbouring a guilty feeling. When he thought of what had occurred very recently, that very night in his life, he could not help but feel happy. The joyous tapestry of experience that night with Anita was marred by a sudden sense of guilt...it seemed to represent a forbidden edge like a border at the end of a sari!

What sort of a person is Anita? A scared woman definitely. She is a creeper who needs my support. What a beautiful clinger! Why did she seek me? It was the most natural and awesome experience! As natural as a bud blooming unnoticed! I swear to take care of you all my life and protect you from all hazards. I shall woo you. I shall marry you. Anita, will you marry me? These were Ganesh's private thoughts at the moment.

'Ganesh! Ganesh!'

'Yes, Monika?'

'Have you had dinner?'

'Yes.'

'Then let's walk down to Nehru Park. Come with me.'

'Why?'

'To talk to you alone.'

Ganesh did not like being alone with her. He was scared of being alone with Monika. He was worried because he had been lying to her. He wanted to escape from Monika and be with his own thoughts. How was he going to achieve that? The secret was tormenting him. *Anita is alone. All alone in her room. She shouldn't be left alone...*

'Moni, can I ask something? If you don't mind or take it amiss?'

'Why not? Shoot.'

'It's very late at night. Let me stay over here tonight. I can use the couch in the living room. Give me a book. I feel there is imminent danger in a girl like you staying alone in this house. Your dad has died under mysterious circumstances. You are my client and your safety is of prime concern to me. That's why I came looking for you. In fact, I would advise you not to roam around alone for a few days. You must obey me implicitly for the next few days. You must follow my instructions to the T. Please don't take it otherwise.'

How many lies!

Monika said, 'Ganesh, you are truly a gem. Wait, let me get you a bed. You can stay here for as long as you please. I have no worries. I can handle a thousand Anitas and more.'

I'm unable to manage one Anita, he thought.

She brought him books, a mattress and water in a glass jug. She showed him the location of the restroom. She told him to not shy away from asking for anything that he might need or require. He thanked her. She showed a keen interest to chat with him. Ganesh pretended to be sleepy. She prattled on for some time, and then mercifully left him alone.

Can Anita hear all this? he wondered.

He could hear Monika brushing her teeth. She was humming to herself. She stopped humming, walked, stood, and opened the window...Hesitated, pondered for a few seconds, and then softly called out: 'Ganesh!'

Ganesh, who had heard all of it and understood the intention clearly, shut his eyes tight and did not reply. Her tone caused alarm bells to ring in his mind. The alarm was a warning to Ganesh, not to Monika.

Why did he wake up later that night? When he thought of it again, all he could do was thank God, who had kept his internal antenna alert.

The moment he opened his eyes, his body was buzzing with excitement, alert and sharp with adrenaline. He could sense someone standing very close. He couldn't see the figure clearly in the glimmering darkness, but could sense it to be a tall figure.

Ganesh held his breath. The stranger approached slowly and raised his right hand...

What was he carrying in his hands? One single blow and...

Ganesh escaped by rolling over. He pulled the intruder's legs. Both rolled over noiselessly on the carpet. It was a blind fight. He could hear the intruder's heavy breathing. Ganesh grabbed his only chance and punched the intruder. He knew the punch had connected because his clenched fist hurt from the impact. The intruder tried to get away. Ganesh pounded him. He was very close, so Ganesh attempted to switch on the light to see him better. The intruder blocked that move, tackled Ganesh and sent him sailing down. He kicked Ganesh with his boots. When the next kick landed, Ganesh held the boot tight. He twisted the ankle with a mighty force.

It must have hurt the intruder badly, but he didn't let

out a scream or a sound. As a last-ditch attempt, he tried using his weapon to strike Ganesh. But it missed, and hit the edge of the chair. Ganesh had moved away. He wondered who the intruder could possibly be. *Must switch on the light...*Ganesh thought, and rushed to the switch board, but the intruder was already gone. There was a single boot on the floor as proof of the scuffle.

The night was still. Ganesh had a blood stain on his shirt. He touched his face, searching for the wound. He thought of the two women sleeping upstairs undisturbed. Their doors were shut and the hum of the air conditioners must have drowned the noise of the scuffle.

'What kind of a guard am I?' Ganesh scolded himself. He worried for Anita. He climbed the stairs carefully, ensuring that he made no noise, rapped her door softly and called out gently, 'Anita!'

After the third call, an alarmed and tremulous voice replied, 'Who is it?'

'Ganesh,' he responded.

The door opened after a small pause. Anita was in a negligee.

'Anita, you are not in any danger, right?'

'Nothing. I had closed all the doors and—My god! What is this blood on your forehead?'

'Someone attacked me now. We fought and most of it is his blood actually.'

Anita switched on a light. 'Look at yourself in the mirror,' she said.

His forehead had a bigger gash than he had imagined.

Anita fetched some antiseptic. She sat him down, cleaned his wound and tied a bandage. 'Ganesh, are you all right?'

'Anita—thank you,' he leaned his head back and took a good look at her. He could see her breasts through the transparent negligee which was practically covering his face. She was standing that close and bending down in concern.

'I'm sorry! Instead of protecting you, I am getting treated for my wounds by you. But...'

'But?'

'One can afford to battle with the world to be nursed by you!'

Anita responded, 'I'm sorry that you are wounded because of me.'

Ganesh looked at himself in the mirror again. She had tied a giant-sized bandage.

'Do you need sleeping pills?'

'No. I must keep watch. Did you forget that?'

'Your watch over us can stop for tonight.'

'No. I need to stay awake tonight. I can't sleep anymore.'

'If you can't sleep, why don't you stay with me here and keep me company?'

'Sure, Anita. Anything for you...I am willing to be with you forever...always!'

He looked up, held her tight and turned her towards him.

SIX

'Hmmm! Not yet...' was Inspector Rajesh's response to Ganesh's question, 'Have you found Govind yet?'

'Are you a lawyer?'

'Yes, the family lawyer.'

'The description that they gave of Govind is insufficient. Medium height, wheatish complexion, khaki shirt—what sort of a description is this?'

'Any photo?'

'I have tried hard to get a photo from them. But I am unable to. By the way, what's that injury on your forehead?'

'I hurt myself.'

'Where?'

Ganesh did not reply.

'Did you find out what sort of a person Govind is?'

'Very sketchy details....The other servants are way too scared to speak to the police. They are concerned the police may associate them with the murder. They are all sure that he left with Mr. Sharma. The money is missing, Mr. Sharma is murdered and Govind is on the run, but...'

'But?'

'There are certain aspects of the case that don't fit in, some discrepancies. Do you smoke?'

10:15

10:16

A minute ticked by with the ritual of lighting cigarettes, a shared moment.

'Please continue,' prompted Ganesh.

'What's your interest in this?'

'As the family lawyer I'd like to cooperate as much as possible with the police.'

'Do you have any new information, Mr. Ganesh?'

'It depends on how far your investigation has progressed.'

Rajesh flicked the ash.

'Not much....We caught someone who matched Govind's description. But we found it wasn't him. Also, a man who commits such a heinous crime will certainly follow a pattern. He will be in hiding for a few days. He will visit his native town or village. He will try to hide in a city. Later he will surface to spend the stolen money. That's when it will be easy for us to nab him. He will go overboard on shopping sprees on unrelated and irrelevant things. When one gets an unexpected booty, one needs the smartness to spend it well too, eh?'

'You said certain things don't fit in this case. Could you share them with me?' asked Ganesh.

'First, a whole day...Sharma and Govind started on a Wednesday. We found the body on Friday evening. Doctors have fixed the time of death as late Thursday night or early hours of Friday in the autopsy report. A whole day is unaccounted for. Sharma's body was found in Ridge Road. It is nowhere en route between Hissar and Sharma's house. Secondly, we found a lot of whip-lash marks on Sharma's body. If the motive was just theft, why inflict such a cruel punishment?'

'Whip lashes?'

'Yes. On the whole body....But from our investigations, we know Govind to be a soft, non-violent person, polite—he's been with the family for the past twenty years.'

'Then, give up searching for Govind. There's a possibility that the answer to the murder could be in Sharma's personal life. You should ferret that out.'

'He seems to have had no professional or business enemies. He did not cheat anyone. He made his money by rigorous hard work. His family life in general seems to be normal. He lost his wife early, and then remarried a young, beautiful woman. So, why have you come to me?'

'There is a small complication in Sharma's will. I need a death certificate. I came to ask for that. Now, did you say whip lashes?'

'Yes, scars, bruises, weals...Why?'

'Someone has punished Sharma in an execution-style killing...'

'Why?'

Ganesh thought for a while and said, 'Thank you, Inspector! If I come up with anything I'll keep you posted.'

'I need Govind's photo somehow.'

'Let me try. I'll take leave of you now.'

When Ganesh called Anita, Bhaskar came on the line. He was informed that Anita was sleeping. When Bhaskar was about to hang up, Ganesh said, 'One moment, Bhaskar.'

'Yes?'

'Where were you last night?'
'I was at home. Why do you ask?'
'Can I meet you? I need to talk to you.'
'I'm a little busy today. Can we meet tomorrow?'
'Ok. I'll come tomorrow,' said Ganesh. But after hanging up, he directly rushed to Anita's house. He drove the car so fast that he reached Vasant Vihar in less than fifteen minutes. He walked quietly into the house.

Bhaskar gave him a startled look. 'Didn't you say you would come tomorrow?'

'I came today...Why are you limping, Bhaskar? What happened to your leg?'

'While I was about to get on to a bus I slipped and sprained it.'

'Shouldn't you have been careful?'

'Hello lover boy!' greeted Monika, wearing a mini skirt paired with a transparent checked shirt. She seemed to have taken extra care with her hair.

She descended the stairs gracefully. Ganesh walked towards her. She held on to his shoulders, took a strong grip and jumped down the last few steps. Her mini skirt flew up once and her thighs flashed.

'Ganesh, do you know the twist dance?'
'No.'
'Jerk, or Shaker, or Mickey?'
'All I know is hand fighting. Judo, karate,' replied Ganesh, staring hard at Bhaskar.

'What happened to your forehead? Are you hurt?'
'I practised fighting with another fellow yesterday.'

'A fight?!'

'Yes.'

'You mean fisticuffs, like in Hollywood movies?'

'Exactly.'

'Why?'

'Just like that! For fitness!'

'You are a strange person. What happened to the will anyway?'

'I'm looking into it. Where's Anita?'

'She is having her bath. If you wait for a few moments she'll change and be with you.'

'Hello, Mr. Ganesh!'

He looked up.

'She has arrived,' commented Monika.

Monika, Bhaskar, that house, the murder, Govind: all of these paled into insignificance for Ganesh at that moment. For the first time since he had met her, Anita had dressed with care. Ganesh's eyes met Anita's. Their shared intimacy and the secret of it brought an instant glow and joy. Anita had just had her bath; her face, fresh as a flower, was soft with water droplets still clinging to her skin, bearing testimony that she had recently stepped out of the bathroom.

'Anita, how are you?' asked Ganesh.

'Am just about okay, thank you.'

'What's wrong with you, Anita?' asked Monika.

'Yesterday a stranger attempted to kill me. If lawyer Ganesh had not turned up, I would have died of fear!'

'What!' exclaimed Monika. It was evident from her tone

that she was itching to pick a quarrel. 'Ganesh, why didn't you tell me? What did you tell me? Why?'

'It was for your own good,' said Ganesh, grinning sheepishly.

'You rogue! You bastard! You double-crossing, stinking, stupid...' Monika screamed at him in her fluent American English. Throwing a glass jar at him, she quickly left the room in a huff. On her way out she said, 'I dismiss you. We have no relationship. We have nothing in common, we are quits!'

Ganesh smiled at Anita pathetically.

'Come up,' she said.

He accompanied her. She asked him to sit. 'Why was Monika angry?'

'I lied to her last night to make her believe that I had come here just for her. Today you called my bluff.'

'Ganesh, why should you lie? Why should you be scared to be with me?'

'Anita, I wish to marry you this minute,' said Ganesh with sudden passion.

'I'm not ready for another marriage, Ganesh. I need to dispose of all my wealth first. I need to get poor...I need mental peace. Let's leave it at that. But why do you suspect Bhaskar?'

Ganesh sat down. 'Why do you think I suspect Bhaskar?'

'I heard you questioning him.'

'Anita, there is a mystery shrouding your husband's death. I am concerned for your welfare and security. Within ten days of your husband's death, an attempt was made on your life. Let's presume for a moment that it was Govind who murdered your husband. If his motive was money, what is the motive for attempting to kill you and me? Also...' Ganesh hesitated. He deliberated whether to tell her or not.

'Also...?'

'The way your husband died...there is a complexity in it...'

'What?'

'His body had whip-lash injuries.'

'God! Who told you?'

'Inspector Rajesh.'

'He never told me this. He was whipped?'

'You actually identified your husband's body. Did you not notice it?'

'He was covered with a sheet. I only looked at his face. I wasn't eager to look at him for too long.'

'I understand.'

'Ganesh, who would want to kill me...?'

'Who will benefit by your death?'

'Oh! No! Only Monika.'

'That's what the will says....But it is not Monika, if I know her.'

'I too know her. It's definitely not her.'

'Then who? Let me figure that out. I'm generally a lazy person. But when I develop an interest in an issue, I do not stop till I resolve it. This murder has grabbed my interest and attention. In fact, I might have been grievously hurt or killed in yesterday's altercation. Please answer my question after careful thought. This Bhaskar…what do you think of him?'

'He is a talented person. Smart, but a coward. He is generally scared. He cannot be associated with the murder at all.'

'Govind?'

'He always tagged along with my husband like a valet and bodyguard. He was like a wall flower and so quiet that I hardly noticed him. Who else do you have in mind?'

'Some more—with names, without names…'

'Am I in the list?'

Ganesh smiled. 'Anita! What is this? Would I suspect you? I'm on this case only for you, and working hard to protect you.'

When Ganesh came down, he found Bhaskar standing near the steps.

'Bhaskar, I am going to ask a straight question for which I need a straight answer.'

Bhaskar was quiet.

'Wasn't it you who tried to attack me last night?'

'No. You are an amateur. You have a fanciful mind.'

'Where were you last night?'

'Playing cards in my club. I have eight to ten people as eye witnesses. But who are you to even question my whereabouts or me? I'm not obliged to answer you in any way.'

'Bhaskar, just remember this. My name is Ganesh and no one has hit Ganesh and escaped the consequences ever!'

'My name is Bhaskar. Anyone who suspects me on silly grounds will end up in grief.'

'Take care of Anita for me.'

'You can do that better, for you are around to wag your tail when whistled for and grab a crumb when it is thrown your way.'

Bhaskar had barely finished with the allegations when he was bashed on his jaw. His spectacles fell off. He rubbed his jaw. He checked his mouth to see if he was bleeding. He picked up the fallen spectacles from the carpet and wiped them clean before wearing them. Ganesh took a classic karate defence position with his arms spread wide, waiting for Bhaskar to retaliate.

Bhaskar said, 'I will not fight with you, but I will surely remember this. I have friends. They will take care of you. Go! Check if Monika is back and work on her too...You have too many spoils on hand!'

Ganesh pounced on him again, but Bhaskar moved away. Ganesh saved himself from falling on the ground by balancing carefully. He straightened himself and paced deliberately towards Bhaskar. Bhaskar smiled and said: 'Truth! Truth always tastes bitter!'

'Your blood will taste sour and bitter for you now!' threatened Ganesh.

'I have plenty of friends. So, easy, lawyer! Easy! You cannot dream of buying classy furniture like this, so chill and don't break it.'

Ganesh couldn't contain his rage; he hurled himself at Bhaskar and held on to his neck.

'Ganesh!' Anita's voice pierced through his cloud of rage. Ganesh stopped his attack immediately.

'Mrs. Sharma, your lawyer is creating a lot of havoc in our house,' commented Bhaskar wryly and dusted his clothes.

'What is this fight about, Bhaskar?'

'I did not raise even a finger at him, Mrs. Sharma!'

'Your secretary is going to end up as dead meat in my hands,' growled Ganesh.

'What did he say?'

'I shared some home truths!' said Bhaskar.

'Forget it, Anita!'

'Ganesh, isn't it enough that we've had a lot of chaos in the past few days?'

'Anita! This secretary does not know how to communicate. Be careful with him. That's all I can say as of now.'

'Exactly my opinion about your lawyer, Mrs. Sharma.'

'You step out and then...!' threatened Ganesh. At the same time, he wondered why he was behaving childishly. Did Bhaskar's statement carry a grain of truth? Why should the truth provoke him? There had to be some mistake! Lots of guilt! Ganesh thought of moving away from Anita. 'I shall meet you in the evening, Anita.'

'I may not be around. I need to step out this evening.'

Though he was badly tempted, he refrained from asking where she was going.

'Let's meet tomorrow then,' said Ganesh.

Bhaskar had already left the room.

SEVEN

That night, Ganesh stayed up for a long time and kept writing in his diary. He was writing and striking out most of it. His mental gears were churning busily. They kept crossing paths; they bloomed like flowers, got all tangled up and then kept twirling more and further more.

He thought. He stared at the telephone. He dialled Anita's number.

It continued ringing without response; he got vexed and hung up. Immediately it sprung to life and rang.

'This is Ganesh here.'

Monika blasted him: 'How much do I owe you, Ganesh? I shall settle your account.'

'It cannot be settled so easily. Where are you calling from?'

'From your granddad's house…'

'He is in heaven. Is everything well there?'

'Ha, ha and ha! What a sense of humour!'

'Listen, Monika. Please listen. I know enough of psychology. Do you know why you are calling me now? You want to make peace with me!'

'Wrong! I don't wish to see you in person. So I am calling you over the phone. You are a…'

'Strong words, my dear girl! Are you certain you don't want to see me?'

'Not in this life.'

'OK. I'm coming over right away...'

'No admission.'

'Are you alone?'

'Yes. I came home just now. I had been out with a dear friend...A dear boyfriend!'

'Good...Monika, will you do a small favour to this friend of yours?'

'No, I will not.'

'What you need to do is...'

'No. Ask Anita when she returns...'

'Monika, I'm still your lawyer. I work day and night for your welfare and to protect you.'

'Where do you work from? Out of Anita's bedroom?'

'Strong words, partner...What should I do now? Am on my knees now...'Will you forgive me please?' is the question I need to ask you. Should I send you roses too?'

'Ganesh, stop flattering me! What do you want? Just get on with that.'

'I need to search your dad's room, then Anita's room.'

'Ok, but I shall be with you throughout.'

'OK,' he agreed.

'This is my dad,' she pointed to a garlanded snap on the table. He was wearing an Indian-style coat without a collar. Not much hair on his head...He had back combed what was left on both sides. A broad forehead, thick eyebrows and very thin lips; his demeanour indicated that he was determined to have his way.

The room was dusty, indicating that no one had entered

it for at least a week. Ganesh pulled open the table's drawers. There were a few pens, a stapler, a cheque book, an appointment diary (he riffled through it and found it unused) and a few papers.

A *Hindustan Times* was on the table. Ganesh looked at the date of the paper. It was the 19th. He threw it away, picked it again. What was the date again? The 19th; the date seemed to bother him.

'Do you have any photo albums?'

'Why?'

'I need to check for Govind's photograph.'

'Let me see.'

The cupboard had plenty of business management books. The wardrobe had many suits and a few dressing gowns. Monika threw the things around her haphazardly.

'Who has the keys to the metal safe?'

'It may be with Anita.'

No photo or diary was found.

'You've messed up everything,' said Monika.

'You are the one who did it. But I couldn't find anything useful. Can I take this photograph?'

'Why do you need my dad's photo?'

'Just like that.'

Monika asked, 'Shall we search Anita's room?'

'What if Anita returns?'

'I shall keep a watch from the window. If we hear the sound of the car, we shall stop searching.'

'Where has she gone by car?'

'I do not know. She did not tell me. We don't talk to each other.'

'Did she go alone?'
'With Bhaskar.'
'That's great!'
'Come, let's search her room.' Monika showed a keen interest to enter Anita's room.

Even in her absence, Anita's room bore her indelible mark and presence. Her trademark traits were all over the room. A few lines scribbled on paper were pinned loosely to the wall:

Spring may go away, but flowers will bloom again!
Beauty will fade and youth will never return!

What a verse! Her bed was neatly made. A tasteful Bombay Dyeing bedsheet was spread on it. Some books were kept near the table (Kabir's writings and Tagore's translations featured). On the wall was a photograph of a young girl surrounded by younger boys. It was Anita when she was seven.

The table had some special yellow customized paper. It could be her favourite colour. Her kajal container had a strange unique shape. The table drawers were all locked. Her sandals were soft velvet moccasins, with many sequins studded on them. They reminded Ganesh of her soft legs and feet. Surprisingly, the bathroom had a very limited cosmetic range; but every item had the tag of a superlative high-quality brand. The glass wall unit had a tiny beautiful doll collection. The wardrobe had numerous saris, mostly in shades of yellow and blue. The saris were not at all dressy but spoke of quality, taste and money. Did she not wear salwar kameezes? A large number of well-tailored blouses were hanging in an orderly fashion. He tried to move them in search of hidden closets.

'What could be in the drawers?' asked Monika.

'They are locked.'

'No keys?'

'I can open them without keys. All I need is a nail.'

'I'll get you a nail.'

'Also keep that watch by the window. Let me know if anyone enters.'

Ganesh opened the drawer effortlessly. The first one had a diary. The first page had the inscription 'Anita—Personal' on it. He did not attempt to read it. There were three insurance policies. All of them were Sharma's. He checked the value of the policies. Their total value was three and a half lakhs. In all three policies, the beneficiary's name had been recently altered to Anita Sharma. There were also a few papers related to the policies.

The next drawer had some random stuff.

Suddenly, 'it' caught his eye. He was startled. Immediately, he shut the drawer.

Another had a pretty green photo album. He opened it. The first page was the engagement photo of Anita and Sharma, wearing huge garlands. The other pages had more photos of the two love birds in hilly areas, boats, resorts, airports, waterfalls, parties; the two of them cooing in various settings.

Plenty of photos and so many people....Monika also appeared in a few. She was much younger; she had huge rings dangling from her ears and long hair. She appeared to have changed so much!

'Monika, come here for a minute.'

'What?'

'Take a look at this whole album. I need just one photo from this. I need Govind's photo. Is he in any one of these? Hurry!'

Monika riffled through it quickly.

'This is he,' she pointed at one.

'I need Govind.'

'This is Govind.'

Govind was standing nervously, very close to his boss but behind him. He had crinkled his forehead because the sun was directly on his face. He had closely cropped hair, was wearing a white shirt and had a thin moustache. He was just a few steps behind Sharma, partly hidden by him.

Ganesh quickly removed that photo from the album and pocketed it. He closed the album shut and replaced it in the same drawer.

'Are there no letters?' asked Monika.

'Plenty...There is even a diary.'

'Let's see...'

'No. Let's not. It won't be fair.'

'Is it fair to break open the drawers? I must see them.'

They heard the honk of a car horn and she wailed, 'Oh! No!'

'Hurry up! Switch off the lights! Move out of the room...' He instructed.

When Anita and Bhaskar entered, Ganesh was sitting in the living room, seemingly unaware of their entry. He was glancing at a weekly.

'Hello, Mr Ganesh!'

'Hello, Anita! You trust Bhaskar enough to go out with him. I don't think it's wise or fair!'

'Where is Monika?'

'She doesn't talk to me. She is inside but doesn't acknowledge me. Just answers questions cursorily from her room.'

'Why have you come here?'

'For your safety. To keep a watch. To save you from villains,' he made the statement with a meaningful glare at Bhaskar.

The drawer had not been locked again. She shouldn't try to open it now. She should not come to know that he had been searching her drawer.

He had still not calmed down or recovered from the shock of seeing 'it' there. His heart was beating fast. He could not focus on what people around him were saying. Various thoughts were swirling around in his head.

'Ganesh, are you going to sleep here tonight?' asked Bhaskar. 'Yes.'

'I don't think it is required of you,' said Bhaskar.

'You shouldn't be the person telling me this.'

When Anita left for her room, his palpitation grew further. *Would she go near the table? Only if she had to write something would she have to go near the table. Would she plan to write anything this late in the night? It's a mistake that I saw 'it'. No, it's actually good that I saw it. I need to be careful from now on. Bhaskar, Anita or Monika...Careful about whom? Or could it be a random fourth person, a total stranger who could have attacked him from outside? Could be a he or she?* thought Ganesh.

'Ganesh, please come up,' called Anita.

(She must have discovered. She has found out that I searched her room. What is she going to ask? What convincing answer can I give?)

She was sitting near her dressing table. She was removing her necklace. She was nowhere close to the other table.

'Ganesh, have you got any information?'

'About what?'

'You have been investigating his murder...'

'I met the police officer. Everybody suspects Govind. I also think it must be my first task to find Govind. I think the description given to the police is not sufficient. They are asking for a photo. Don't you have any photo of his at all in this house?'

'As far as I can recollect, nothing. I don't remember having seen his photograph.'

Ganesh felt his pocket for the photo that he had pinched from the album.

(Why is she lying? Has she never seen the album? Anita's first lie! Are they all lying? Monika? What was her first lie?)

Anita was changing from her sari into her negligee. She was changing casually in front of him with no shyness or hesitation, like it was a routine activity. But there was nothing casual in her curves and the skin that flashed while she changed; these stimulated Ganesh's hormones tremendously and jangled his nerves.

Anita lay down on her bed and stretched her limbs and body like a contented kitten. What a transparent gown she was wearing!

'Ganesh, come here please!'

(Don't go! Don't! Have you forgotten? What did you see in that drawer, Ganesh? What did you see? A four-pronged whip!)

'Good night, Anita!'

Ganesh walked out of that room without a glance behind.

EIGHT

As soon as he stopped his car in front of his house, Ganesh noticed a man walking towards him. From his height, weight, stature and clothes, Ganesh tried to gauge the man's social status.

Ganesh locked the car door, showing no indication of having noticed the person. He started to hum casually while taking the key out of his pocket to open the grill gate...

'Just a minute!' the man said.

Ganesh turned to look at him. He wasn't all that good-looking; he was crafted to fit the bill for assignation of violent acts. He wore a leather jacket, a loose metal strap watch; the sideburns of his wavy hair were long, and he had a luxuriant moustache. Ganesh barely noticed all this, but registered just one vital point: he was definitely ten kilos heavier than Ganesh.

'What do you want?' Ganesh asked.

'I need to talk to you.'

'About what?'

'It's about some business, open the door.'

'What business?'

'I shall tell you. Open the door.'

'I am Ganesh.'

'Your name is Ganesh. I know that very well. Hey, dude! Please open the door. Luck awaits you.'

Ganesh hesitated to allow him in. But the stranger walked into the house like he belonged there. He switched on the lights by groping on the wall. The flood of light made it easier to take a closer look at him. But it did not improve his visage; he was no eye-candy. The stranger plonked himself heavily on the sofa, made himself comfortable and instructed, 'Why don't you turn the fan on?'

'What do you want?' asked Ganesh.

'I will ask that question. What do you want?'

'For what?'

'To forget everything…To step away from this case… To stay away.'

'Which case?'

'You are a lawyer with hardly any cases. You just have one case. Anita.'

'Anita? Oh! Mrs. Sharma.'

'Mrs. Sharma! Had that man been alive, he would have slaughtered you.'

'It's because he isn't alive that I—'

'Don't talk too much. State what you need,' he slid his hands inside his trouser pockets.

'Why?'

'To R-E-M-O-V-E yourself from the mockery of this case. You need to completely extricate yourself from it. You shouldn't even step near the house. You should not meet that girl Monika. That's it. Clear out. Shut shop. How much do you want?'

'Just one question: who are you?'

'A friend.'

'Whose?'

'Right now, yours. I am here to save you from trouble. Tell the number. I'll write a cheque for you. How many thousands? Go on...'

'What's your name?'

'Shastri.'

Ganesh laughed. 'Shastri, huh? Try again, Shastri.'

'Don't laugh. Tell me how much money you need.' He pulled out a Syndicate Bank cheque book and looked ready for the task.

'If the cheque bounces...?'

'Do you need cash? I shall arrange it in about half an hour. Tell me the amount.'

'I need time to think,' said Ganesh.

'What is there to think? Don't you know to count beyond hundred?'

'Shastri! Get out!'

'What? Did you take a good look at me? How dare you say get out? Take a closer look at me.' Shastri stood up and flexed his muscles like a contestant in a body-building pageant.

Ganesh repeated, 'Get out!'

'Hey! Do you have a death-wish?'

'Shastri, look here, this is the way. Way to exit. Do you know the spelling of exit?'

Shastri threw a punch. Ganesh ducked and the punch hit the edge of the sofa. He must have hurt himself. Shastri got angrier, like a mad bull elephant. He pounced on Ganesh, who swerved and ran around the sofa. Shastri stretched his arms wide and approached Ganesh as though he was about to trap a chicken. He pulled out a knife.

Ganesh cried out, 'Chotelal! Chotelal!', loud enough for Chotelal, who was seated in the cycle shop in the opposite house, to hear!

Chotelal ran inside, grabbed the hand holding the knife and shook it off. He hit Shastri's back with his knees. Both Ganesh and Chotelal together pounded Shastri.

After the entire scuffle they made Shastri sit straight, tidied him a little, offered him a bottle of soda, put his cheque book into his pocket; then Ganesh asked him, 'Shastri! Tell me now.'

Shastri asked, 'What?' But he was practically voiceless. He couldn't even get up.

'Shastri, I can lodge a police complaint and pack you off to jail right away. There are so many witnesses. All of you please disperse! There isn't a show going on here! Don't gape! Go...mmm...Now tell me,' said Ganesh.

'What do you need to know?'

'Who sent you here?'

'No one.'

'Chotelal, call the police. Call the flying squad. They will resolve this. Tell them, he entered my house and hit me. He tried to stab me. Look at the blood; my shirt is torn... Shastri, for the last time, who sent you here?'

'Bhaskar,' said Shastri.

'Thank you, Shastri. Would you like to have another soda?'

The next morning, at around ten o'clock, Ganesh made three phone calls.

The first, to Inspector Rajesh: 'Inspector Rajesh? Ganesh here...do you remember? I need a small favour from you...I need the dead Sharma's post-mortem report. Whom should I ask?...A moment—let me note it down. Yes please, noted...Nothing really. I just want to see the report. Just once, I request you to allow me. Did you arrest Govind?... No? It's tough...No, sir. I need a certificate. That's all my interest is...I shall come and meet you. Bye.'

The second, to the Indian Air Force headquarters: 'Air Force Headquarters? Extension 239, please...Squadron Leader Ramalingam...Thank you...Ramalingam! Ganesh here...(A smile) Oh yes...Oh yes. How is Prem? You are all big shots...Not at all! By the way, I need some information from you. It may appear strange to you...This is the matter...I need information about a Flight Lieutenant Raja. R-a-j-a; R for Radhika, A for Angela, J for Janaki, A for Aruna...(Laughter) Raja...Someone informed me that Flight Lieutenant Raja died in a transport flight in Agra a few years ago. I need to confirm it...Not all that. A cross check...When will I get the information?...Okay. I shall wait at Vayu Bhavan, this evening at 4.30. Flight Lieutenant Raja...R for...Okay. Thanks.'

The third, to the Overseas Cable Service: 'O.C.S.? Enquiries please...Enquiries? How long will it take a cable to reach America if sent from Delhi? My name is Ganesh. I am a lawyer. Please tell me how long it takes...Thank you very much, Miss! You have a great voice.'

Ganesh combed his hair. He bit into two protein biscuits. He left his home. He reached Bhaskar's house.

'Whom do you need?' asked the servant.

'Isn't Bhaskar around?' asked Ganesh.

'No. He is likely to be in Sharma Saheb's house.'

Ganesh scanned the room keenly while talking to the servant and made mental notes. Bhaskar's room was tidy. He found the book 'The Money Game', a Monarch talcum powder box, a green dustbin, chairs, table, Vivekananda and Hema Malini's pictures.

'Are you his servant?' Group photo...Telephone...

'Yes...and you are?' A tidy single cot...Magazines...

'His friend, coming from Agra.'

'Give me your name. I shall inform him when he comes.'

'I shall call on him myself. What's your name?' Corduroy shoes, black box, steel almirah.

'Ram Swaroop.' Centre of the table had a deck of cards with nude photographs.

'Good name. Ram Swaroop, I need just one minute.'

'Yes, sir!'

'Ten days ago, Bhaskar wrote a letter to me promising to visit Agra. I wasn't in Agra then. I had to leave on an official trip. Did your boss go to Agra?'

'When, sir?'

'Last 18th or maybe 17th...'

'No! He did not go anywhere.'

'Did he not leave Delhi?'

'No! He has been in Delhi continuously for the past four, five months.'

Ganesh came out of Bhaskar's house, got into his car and joined the traffic. Driving slowly, he was reflecting on all that he had heard so far. *Bhaskar, you are that sort of a person, huh? You have lied, is it? You are paying money to remove me from the scene? You are hitting me and hurting me? Why, Bhaskar? Why? I shall find out, no worries*, he ruminated.

The moment Ganesh entered the house in Vasant Vihar, Monika greeted him.

'Hello! You look great. Whom are you trying to impress?' she asked.

'Good morning,' he said shortly.

'Ganesh, how old are you?'

'Add ten years to your age.'

'I love that.'

'Which?'

'I love a man older than me. An experienced guy...'

'You'd love him, I am sure,' he replied. 'But this someone who is older and more experienced is actually in a rush. Where is Anita?'

'You'd like to have her *darshan*? Sorry, she isn't around.'

'That means...?'

'She left last night somewhere. She hasn't returned till now.'

Ganesh looked at his watch patiently.

'Ganesh, I need to share something very important with you,' said Monika.

'Tell me, I'm done here.'

'Yesterday, I got a telephone call. Some strange voice...I don't know his name. He asked if I was willing to sell the company shares that I would get from my father's will. He asked me to meet him at a hotel in Connaught Place at eleven o'clock tonight if I wanted a good price.'

'Was the voice familiar?'

'No. It was unfamiliar.'

'Come. Let's go,' said Ganesh.

An old gramophone from Edison days welcomed them at the hotel entrance. As soon as they entered, the first thing they saw was a strategically placed red bike. The place was filled with smoke. A juke box was screaming. The double bass was going 'Boom, boom!' Hippies, Indian hippies, international hippies, wannabe hippies who were halfway through but were forced to cut their hair because of parental pressure, half hippies—here a hippy, there a hippy, everywhere hippies….

A foreigner wearing wooden clogs, bare-bodied except for a towel around his waist, a Charminar cigarette packet tucked into it; brown hair, wild and unkempt; green eyes shining like twin emeralds, was preaching about the *Gita* to a woman in front of him.

A Bob Dylan song was pervading the room. Ganesh felt terribly out of place in the crowd. They were seated. Monika slowly started drumming on the table.

Ganesh asked loudly, 'Did he ask you to come to this place?'

'Yes,' said Monika.

'We can't talk about anything here. My throat will dry up.'

'Hmmm,' Monika nodded.

The place was scorching with the heat of the youth.

Monika's skirt was riding alarmingly high. Everyone seemed to notice it except her. Ganesh was peering anxiously at the entrance. None of the visitors seemed to be potential candidates for buying shares.

A yippy (an Indian hippy) came to the table and sat down. He said, 'Baby!'

Ganesh looked at Monika. She unhesitatingly said, 'Yeah, sugar doll!'

The yippy turned around and looked at Ganesh, 'Who are you? Are you my dad?'

'Your grand dad,' said Ganesh.

'Hello Gramps! Pleased to meet you!'

Ganesh rubbed his nose with his pinkie. Monika laughed. The guy screwed up his courage, swung his arms around her waist and said, 'Come upstairs. There is a billiards table there!'

Ganesh got up, plucked the yippy off her and threw him away. If you thought the thrown yippy was angry, you would not be wrong. He picked a huge ceramic plate from a waiter's tray and flung it at Ganesh.

Hippies are very modern in very many ways. But apparently their skill at flinging ceramic plates when angry isn't good. The plate hit the turban of Jarnail Singh, a newly married Sardarji who was entering the hotel, accompanied by his equally newly-wed wife. Sardarjis are generally known to love fights. J. Singh was recently married and trying to make an impression on his wife. When relieved of his turban, this Sardarji's anger knew no bounds.

Singh pounced like a flash on the yippy. Some more

hippies joined the fray—Ganesh, Singh, Hippy 1, Hippy 2, Waiter, Singh, and Hippy 3—the melee upset the peace of the hotel.

Someone sat on the ice-cream. Someone was drenched in Gold Spot. Monika climbed on a table and started looking for Ganesh. The international hippy (Charminar touting and towel-clad) continued to expound on the *Gita* to his pupil. The hotel manager clung to the telephone, scampered under the table and called the Parliament Street police station....

NINE

Ganesh escaped with Monika from the brawl through the hotel kitchen into an alley, crossed a tailor's shop and a few other small shops, and ran to his parked car.

Monika had lost one of her sandals and her mini skirt had been torn into a micro-mini. So she had to run with effort.

She started laughing as soon as she reached Ganesh's room.

'Why are you laughing?'

'Your nose! Ha ha! On your nose...'

Ganesh looked at the mirror. There was some yellow icky stuff on his nose.

He licked it off his fingers and said appreciatively, 'Marmalade.'

She laughed louder. Ganesh asked, 'Monika, why did you lie to me?'

'What?'

'That someone called you to the hotel...Wasn't that a lie?'

'Yes.'

'So why did you lie?'

'That's because I love you,' she replied.

'Let's argue about your love later. Here, wear this.'

Ganesh's Armour shirt fitted her and looked good on

her. As she sewed the rent on her skirt with a needle and thread, she gulped down the tea that was fetched by the boy from the tea-shop. Ganesh changed his shirt. He took one long look at her and said, 'You look pretty. You have left out a button. You are deliberately not wearing it. Are you attempting a *'Mera Naam Joker'* look?'

Not understanding the reference, she looked puzzled. But she had the good grace to blush and shyly buttoned up.

'Ganesh, I'm going to ask you a direct question. You need to answer in one word—yes or no.'

'I know what you are going to ask. The answer is no.'

'What is my question?'

'You know that quite well.'

'But you wouldn't know…you (hesitantly)…that night…'

'Don't ask! Don't you dare ask!'

'With Anita…in that room…'

'You want to know what I talked about. Generally about your dad…'

'What did you do?'

'Come again…'

'What did you do?'

'My dear girl, you have got me wrong. I haven't thought of anyone other than you—other than Monika Sharma—not even in my dreams. Never have I thought of anyone else.'

She didn't seem to be satisfied with his dismissive professing of empty words. 'Ganesh, are you like Lord Krishna?'

'Why?'

'Why do women fall all over you?'

'Is that so? Mons, I am like a pure dewdrop. I specialize in virgins! Only time can explain the truth of this statement. Let me share a Sardarji joke with you: Gurumukh Singh travelled for the first time from his village to Jalandhar—'

'Burn your joke! What do you plan to do now?'

'I shall drop you at your house.'

'No thanks, I shall leave alone.'

'I have become completely embroiled in the tangle of your dad's murder.'

'Isn't it Govind's doing? There is no doubt about that.'

'There are plenty of doubts.'

'Just a moment! Why have you changed tracks? Your job was to analyze the will...'

'There are two reasons. First: Presently, I have no other work. I am caught up with the mystery of your house. Second: Women. Two beautiful women, Anita and Monika. Both seem to hate each other tremendously. Wait, I'm not yet done. The second reason would be the "why" of your dad's murder. If we presume the murderer to be Govind, there are plenty of questions that arise; can you guess?'

'What questions?'

'There were a lot of random injuries on your dad's body. Why? Both Anita and I were attacked last night. Why? It has been generally gathered that Govind is a loyal servant. Where did he go? If he committed the murder, there are other things that don't fit. Then there is this strange behaviour of Bhaskar, the lies that he has stated. Bhaskar does not approve that I am involved in this case. Your step mother Anita is vehement that she wants to renounce your father's property. A certain over-emphasis is noticeable in her renunciation. Also, there is a sense of artificiality in your house. There doesn't seem to be enough grief for your dad. There is no progress after the death. No one is showing any keenness in his estate, paying taxes, setting records straight or dividing the shares of the property—other than you. There must be one simple answer that would clarify all these doubts. I am searching for that answer.'

'You think I'll get my money only after you find that answer?'

'Yes.'

'That's fine! How many days will it take?'

'I do not know. I have decided to cross-check the validity of all the information I have received from the day of your dad's death till date. Facts, statements and eye witness accounts should be validated. Only then can I make an effort to piece them together into a big picture.'

'Ganesh, do you suspect Anita?'

'Anita? Yes…and…?'

'How about Bhaskar and me?'

'I suspect everyone. I suspect no one. Let's start. I need to go up to the Air Force headquarters.'

'Why?'

'It's related to this case.'

'What's the connection between the Air Force and my dad's death?'

'All of you lie completely. Like a swan, I need to decipher the truth from all this.'

'What did I lie about?'

'Just now, you lied about the call and dragged me to that hotel...'

'I have already given you the reason, Ganesh.'

'You mentioned love, right? I remember now. Let's make love next Friday.'

'At times I feel like strangling you with my bare hands.'

After Ganesh had dropped her near the university area to meet a friend, he reached the Air Force headquarters. He felt different from the rest, all uniformed officers. He waited for Squadron Leader Ramalingam. Ganesh had long ago presented a brilliant argument in court in Ramalingam's family litigation and so they were well-acquainted. At times he would seek a favour from Ramalingam, like a bottle of rum from the Air Force mess at subsidized rate. Right now, he sought a different favour.

'Hello Ganesh!' Ramalingam slapped his back.

'Hello sir! How are you?'

'How do I look? I am ready to start a war with Pakistan any time. Don't you see?'

'Are they going to attack us?'

'We are ready. Be seated.'

They sat in a corner at the reception. 'OK, who is this Flight Lieutenant Raja?'

'I have come here to ask you the same question.'

'I don't understand.'

'My question is this. One Flight Lieutenant Raja was supposedly killed in an air crash on a transport flight in Agra. Is that true?'

Anita: A Trophy Wife / 89

'Yes…in 1965, a cargo aircraft crash landed in Agra. Raja was one among the dead.'

Ganesh suddenly felt insanely jealous of Raja.

'Why do you need this information?'

'It pertains to a case. Someone gave this detail. I needed to verify it.'

'That mystery someone who gave the detail—was it a man or a woman?'

'A woman.'

'Ah! I thought so. What happened to that other woman Neeraja? You were going around with her for a while.'

'Oh yes. Neeraja! We send new year greetings to each other…'

'Right now who is on the list…?'

'No one. This is a murder case. An interesting one at that.'

'Give me an account later. I am busy now.'

'I promise to tell you. Thank you.'

'Bye! Be well!'

On an impulse, instead of going to the police station to meet the inspector as planned, Ganesh went to Vasant Vihar. He wondered if Anita would be alone.

Anita had not lied…No…no, she had not lied too much.

He met Meenakshi in the living room.

'Is Anita at home?'

'Yes.'

'Where did she go? Should I ask?' he thought. Monika

wouldn't be back yet. Anita was around...While climbing the stairs, he kept thinking that he would get to know today. It would all be revealed.

Anita had obviously been crying. And then in a rushed, clumsy manner, she had applied compact on her tear-stained face. Her eyes were red-rimmed. She did not greet him as he entered. She merely gazed at him...

He waited.

'Ganesh! How much can I trust you?' she asked after composing herself.

'Why, Anita?'

'I have no one to trust and share. I have nobody...Today I experienced hell: pain, sorrow, shame. I wish it on no one else...'

'What happened?'

'First I must clarify something. Do you suspect me or not?'

'I suspect everyone, Anita.'

'Why do you suspect me?'

'Anita, everyone in this house happens to be lying.'

'Me too?'

'Yes.'

'What lie?'

'You called me the other night. You said someone was trying to murder you. You were waiting outside your house. Your things were strewn around. Your bangles were broken. Clothes torn, every little thing was a staged play!'

Anita's head was bent down.

'Why do you feel that it was staged?'

'I might look like a fool at times. But I am no one's fool. The details that you shared and the details that I noticed in the room were not in sync. You said: "I was reading... The window opened...Thinking it was the breeze I turned around slowly. He was standing..." The weal on your neck looked natural too. But those were lipstick marks...and then those nail scratches...'

Anita kept quiet.

'I understand why you called me. Bhaskar had taught you well. It was his plan. To invite me, to gain my sympathy, to make me spend the night here, and then, to attack me! I would have to conclude that the one who attacked you attempted an attack on me too! To remove me from the scene! I know it was Bhaskar who attacked me the other night. Anita, both you and Bhaskar do not approve of my investigating this case or helping Monika in understanding the will. Bhaskar sent a goon to my place who offered me money to withdraw from the case. You both seem to share some common secret....'

'What secret?'

Was he sharing too much information with her? He wanted to try and extract information from her.

'You are avenging your husband's murder. You are taking Bhaskar's help...'

Anita laughed.

'Take a good look at me, Ganesh. Look at my body. Look at my helpless hands. Look at my piteous strength.'

'I am not talking of brawn here—it's about the mental strength and brain. Anita, I wasn't born yesterday. I am not willing to believe that Govind is the killer. He is behind the scenes...Bhaskar's claim to have been at Agra the other day was a blatant lie. He has not moved out of Delhi. Govind doesn't have a motive to kill. Murder is a crime of passion. Extreme hatred, disappointment, phenomenal anger, temporary cruelty...such base emotions result in murder. Anita, why don't you reveal the truth?'

'What would you like me to tell you? That I took revenge on Sharma? That I arranged Govind's going underground? It's all me? I think you need basic lessons in psychology, Ganesh!'

'Sharma was whipped. Are you aware of it?'

'Is it?'

'Your intonation of those two words contains a lot of latent cruelty. I happened to see a whip in one of the drawers in a table in your room.'

'Is it?'

Ganesh looked straight at her. 'Anita! Who are you? Who are you? Who exactly are you?' were the questions in his eyes. 'I am an innocent person, looking for support,' answered Anita's eyes.

Anita laughed hysterically. It was a trifle loud.

'Ganesh, your surmise is that I and Bhaskar hatched this plan. Please listen to this. Bhaskar came here this morning. Do you know what he told me? "Sharma is dead and gone! Why don't you be my wife?" After making this comment, he removed his spectacles and pushed me on the bed. "I shall ensure that all the money comes to you! Come to me, my queen!" was his invitation. He said that he had spent all these years in this house to do just this, to reach out to me! Today, an opportunity has been created for him. How many lecherous men can I handle, Ganesh? My creator has shaped this body and face and seems to have instilled lust in every man who meets me. I sought only support from you, just support. I have this attractive womanhood thrust on me, which I did not ask for. Just to garner some sympathy from you, I had to lie a bit. Is that a crime? Right from the servant to the secretary, everyone wants to have a piece of me, to attain me. In this piteous context I am looking for a lasting friendship. Would that be expecting too much?'

'Did Bhaskar proposition you?'

'Please believe me. Yes, he did. Call Meenakshi. Ask her what she saw when she entered the room. You think I have joined hands with Bhaskar? Ask Meenakshi!'

'No! I shall leave now.'

'Where are you off to?'

'I'm going to call on Bhaskar. Anita, be patient. I worship you. You know that yourself. I very much wish to believe that you did not lie. Please wait. I must see Bhaskar immediately. I need to resolve this one way or the other.'

'Bhaskar is dangerous!'

'I know, Anita.'

Ganesh was boiling and seething with pent-up anger when he entered his car. He revved the engine and vroomed past, cutting corners. 'Bhaskar! Bhaskar! I'm right behind you! I'm after you! I have understood you clearly. You touched Anita, huh? I'm coming after you. You asked her to yield to you? I'm right there,' he spoke to himself.

Darkness fell on the city. He parked in front of Bhaskar's house, opened the door, slammed it hard and climbed the stairs two steps at a time, turned left, reached Bhaskar's room and kicked the door open...

Ganesh froze at the sight before him. The fan was whirring slowly; a lone bulb was burning; between the cot and table, Bhaskar's spectacles had splintered; a little distance away, Bhaskar was lying diagonally on the ground, definitely dead!

TEN

That was the first time Ganesh had seen a dead body at close quarters.

He had argued for the dead plenty of times. But he had never before met them so intimately. Bhaskar's look had changed completely. With blood pumping through his face, Bhaskar had had an intelligent look. Now, with no blood pumping, his face looked waxy and expressionless, frozen somewhere between fear and surprise. His teeth were bared. His body hadn't suffered any superficial wound. He was wearing a dhoti. He was definitely dead.

Should he touch the body? Hmmm...No! Should he run away?

Ganesh then noticed that Bhaskar was lying in a pool of blood, a red puddle. Ganesh looked around. There was a coat hanging from a nail on the wall. He took one look at the telephone and made his decision.

When he crossed Bhaskar, he was quite scared. Boom! What if Bhaskar stood up suddenly? No. Bhaskar could never get up. He was still lying in the blood. 'Dead!' Ganesh said to himself...

Trring...Trring...

'I am Ganesh. I am calling from 33, Hayley Road. There is a dead man here. He is on the floor...on the floor, in his flat, right inside, in the room, on the floor, on the ground,

33, Hayley Road...first floor, yes; I think it's a murder...I shall not move. I shall wait for you. 33, Thenthees (in Hindi) Thirty-three.'

Bhaskar and Ganesh waited. Ganesh planned his next move. He took another look at Bhaskar. He wondered if Bhaskar was a changeling or a chameleon. Ganesh used the telephone again.

'Inspector Rajesh? Ganesh here. I am calling from Bhaskar's house. Bhaskar is dead.'

'What? When? How?'

'I came to Hayley Road to talk to him. I saw his body. Simple.'

'Have you reported it?'

'Immediately. The flying squad will arrive here any moment.'

'I shall be there now. It's quite puzzling.'

He heard footsteps nearing the room. He had perspired quite a lot! With one eye on the door, Ganesh pulled out his handkerchief to wipe his face. The boy was humming a Hindi song—*Mere samne wali khidki mein*...He was carrying a Tiffin carrier and a new pack of cigarettes.

The boy left the Tiffin carrier on the table. He looked at Bhaskar and Ganesh. The humming came to a grinding halt. The cigarettes slipped from his hands and fell down.

'Woooh!' he wooshed and his eyes popped!

'Don't be scared. This is just a...'

He kept looking down. 'Khoon! Chor!' he started screaming at the top of his voice. He jumped and ran out of the room. Ganesh could hear both his scream and his rushing footsteps down the stairs. He could also hear garbled voices and a crowd gathering on the ground floor. In a perplexing mix, he heard some stray Hindi words. 'In the morning, this is the fellow who came and enquired, Chopraji. He is inside. He is holding something white in his hands. Bhaskar Saheb is on the floor. Blood all over. He is continuing to stand there.'

'Is he still there?'

'Yes. Standing.'

'Is he having a knife in his hands?'

'He has something in his hands.'

'How old does he look?'

'He is tall and fair.'

'Chopraji! Come! Let's take a look.'

The voices gathered strength and courage in number. They started climbing the stairs.

Pheee, the siren screamed. Boots thumped.

'Police!'

Ganesh heaved a sigh of relief. He stepped out of the room, crossed his arms on his chest and waited. How many of them were reaching the first floor?

Voices, footsteps, threats...

An officer was sighted. He looked at Ganesh.

His look had C.R.P.C. stamped all over it.

'Did you call?'

'Yes. My name is Ganesh.'

'Where is the body?'

Ganesh pointed inside.

'Where?'

'Right on the floor.'

'Oh yes.' He hesitated a little.

A constable was pushing a crowd of fifteen people down the stairs.

The inspector pulled out an ink pen from his pocket, shook it a few times. He took his pocket book to note down various details. He licked his thumb, flipped through the pages and stopped at a fresh page. Ganesh was watching him keenly. How many kinds of officers, and with different traits!

'Don't go anywhere!'

The gruffness of his tone indicated that Ganesh was a suspect. 'I shall not move,' he reassured the policeman.

With the constable's help, the inspector moved the table. He walked around Bhaskar once. He noted down the date and time in his pocket book.

'Find out whose house this is.'

'The person staying here is Bhaskar. He is the dead man,' said Ganesh.

'Why did you come here?'

'To meet him.'

'Dost (friend)?'

'Acquaintance.'

The steps were crowded. The boy shouted: 'Saheb. This man had called this morning when my boss was not around.'

'Who are you?'

'I am Bhaskar Saheb's servant.'

Ganesh thought, 'Here comes the knot.' But he

steeled himself with the confidence that he had nothing to fear.

'You wait. I shall talk to you. Then I need to question all of you. Come in, 18.'

Two more officers joined the band. Their shoulder pads had silver stars, and black and red bands. One of them stiffly saluted while the other saluted as if he couldn't care less. All of them—Punjabis—looked strong and ruddy.

Ganesh waited for Rajesh, feeling all eyes focused on him. He tried to look nonchalant. Ganesh suddenly thought of Anita. Some inexplicable fear sent its cold clammy fingers down his spine. Who had killed Bhaskar? Could it be the one who had killed Sharma? Was Anita next on the list? Why was Bhaskar killed? Ganesh had been suspecting Bhaskar, who was conveniently bumped off. Who else is left? Anita, Monika and Govind. Yes. Must be Govind! How could one tell for sure? What kind of an enmity was this? Random murders, all irrelevant? Oh, Anita!

'What is your name?'

'Ganesh.'

'Please give a detailed account of all that you observed.'

Ganesh began his narration like an automaton. Even while he was reciting away, his mind was on Anita. He felt he must call her, warn her.

'Sir, I need to make a call.'

'You cannot use this phone,' said the inspector.

'Not this. Let me go to a shop outside. No big matter. I

need to inform the dead man's boss lady. She is expecting me. She stays alone. I shall be back in a minute.'

The inspector looked at the ASP. He gave it a thought.

'All right. Constable, you accompany him,' he said.

When Ganesh came out of the room, the crowd gathered there riled him with their hateful looks.

'He is the one.'

'They have handcuffed him.'

'He looks like a young man.'

'Send your sister to me,' growled Ganesh and descended angrily. The constable tagged along, apparently glued to him. Vividh Bharathi was blaring from the radio in the shop. Ganesh pulled some small change out and told the shop keeper that he had to make a call. The shop keeper asked, 'What is the number? Let me dial it for you.' He seemed to fear a sneaky STD call.

'Six one double six four three.'

The shopkeeper dialled the number and handed over the receiver to Ganesh.

'Anita?'

She said, 'Yes.' It was definitely her voice.

'Anita, Ganesh here. Something terrible has happened.'

'What is it, Ganesh?'

' Ustad, can you please lower the radio volume? Anita, now listen to me without panic. Bhaskar has been murdered.'

'Bhas...kar?'

'Yes.'

'Ganesh!' Her voice became feeble. 'What are you saying? Really? How did it happen?'

'We shall know soon. I happened to see first. He is dead in his flat. I went to pick a quarrel with him. Tsk... tsk! Now I can't!'

'Ganesh, I am scared. I am truly alarmed. Would you please come here and take me away?'

'Isn't anyone around? Where is Monika?'

'Monika has gone out. Ganesh, please come here straightaway, immediately. I shall confess everything to you. I am terrified. Ganesh, please come right now...'

'Anita, I am caught in a fix. I cannot come right now. They haven't completed the enquiry. I may be able to come in, say, thirty minutes. Don't send the servants away. Where is the car?'

'Monika has taken it. Ganesh, I must talk to you. I need to tell you all....Right now...'

'I shall come there as soon as possible. But don't stay alone. I shall definitely come.'

Another constable came back with a message that Ganesh was required. Ganesh put the phone down, paid up and started to walk towards the house. Her words 'I must tell you all' were ringing in his ears. Did that mean there were details she had left out? What could they be? Would Anita be in the know? When Ganesh returned to the crime scene, Inspector Rajesh had arrived. He greeted the inspector.

'We meet again,' Rajesh told Ganesh.

Ganesh smiled, but Rajesh was grim.

'The ASP is talking to the neighbour. Have you told them all that you observed?'

The neighbour was busy with his tale: 'Sir, a car came and stopped near the house after darkness fell. It was a black Ambassador. Someone got down and went up.'

'How did he look?'

'I did not see his face. He rushed up the stairs. I couldn't see him clearly.'

'How tall was he? Was he this tall?' The inspector pointed at Ganesh.

'Perhaps! Could be his height.'

'Which age bracket?'

'I do not know. I told you already, I did not look at him carefully.'

'Was he driving the car?'

'I think so.'

'What was the car number?'

'I did not notice the car number. The one who got down hurried into the house. I saw him climb the stairs to the left.'

'Did anyone else happen to see him?'

'I saw, sir. I saw the car stop.'

'At what time?'

Ganesh observed the room carefully, searching for clues. The last shelf of the cupboard contained stacked newspapers. The books were arranged neatly by their spines. Ink bottle, bags...his eyes met Inspector Rajesh's. He gestured for Ganesh to come out.

'Why did you come here, Ganesh?' The inspector's tone was rude. Why?

'Quite simple. I came to see Bhaskar.'

'When you came...?'

'Bhaskar was certainly dead when I came in. I can swear on my father.'

'I don't need all that. You see...'

'Mr Ganesh, please come this way,' said the ASP.

'Is this the person?'

'Yes. Him.'

'What is it, sir?' asked Ganesh.

The ASP did not look into his eyes. 'What did he ask you?'

The boy said: 'He asked if Bhaskar had visited Agra last week. He claimed to be his friend. He claimed he lived in Agra. He mentioned that he expected Bhaskar in Agra.'

The ASP looked at Ganesh in a questioning manner. Ganesh cleared his throat.

'I can explain this. Inspector Rajesh knows. I am helping late Mr. Sharma's daughter with his will. Bhaskar claimed to have been in Agra on the day of the murder. I came to check his statement...'

'What is this Agra business, Rajesh?'

'Sir, there is another case related to this. R. K. Sharma was this dead man Bhaskar's boss. On the 18th of last month, near Ridge Road—'

'I know. I get the connection. In other words, Ganesh, you were investigating Sharma's murder, right?'

'Yes, apparently.'

'But who are you to do that? What is this, Rajesh?'

'I'm a lawyer.'

Rajesh coughed in discomfort.

Ganesh continued, 'I needed a proper death certificate. I was suspicious of Sharma's death.'

'We know that Bhaskar was not in Agra, Ganesh,' said Rajesh.

'What did you say your name was?' asked another officer.

'Ganesh: G-A-N-E-S-H.'

'Rajesh, whatever he claims...'

'Is the truth. He is the family lawyer. He had perhaps come to visit Bhaskar.'

'What are you trying to state? That I could have committed this murder? Joke of the day!'

'We are not alleging that. We are just cross-checking. That's it.'

Rajesh went in. The officer who had asked his name checked Ganesh's trouser pockets.

'Should I remove my trousers?' he asked.

'Not necessary,' said the officer. 'Banerji, what is it?'

Banerji, who came out of the room, said, 'Sir, the dead man has been shot. Shot at close range. The bullet is likely to be inside the body. In fact, the gun must have touched his body when he was shot. Not much blood loss. It's all clogged.'

'That's better. Did any one of you hear a gun shot?'

The crowd looked at one another. '*Ai bhai, zara dekhke chalo...*' blared the radio in the shop as if in reply. A scooter without a silencer sped down the road.

'This place is perpetually noisy. So even if he was shot, people could have missed the sound.'

'He must have been caught by surprise when he was shot. Black Ambassador. Are you sure it was a man?'

Ganesh thought of Anita again. 'Please come soon. I shall tell all.' What would she confess?

'Sir, can I leave?'

'Give us your address.'

'I have given it in the statement. I have also given my telephone number.'

Ganesh rushed to his car, gained speed and the tyres screeched on the road. He was reminded of the high speed at which he had raced out of Anita's house a few hours back. 'I need speed,' he muttered; a speed that can consume time.

When he returned to Vasant Vihar , the house was steeped in silence.

Was it too silent? Did the emptiness deliver a warming? He shut the car door gently. The gate was open.

'Meenakshi!'

'Ram!'

'Hello!'

There was no answer. The lights were on.

'Monika!'

Hmmm.

He climbed the stairs gingerly. Another flight of stairs... Another room...Don't go there!

'Anita! Anita!'

Anita's door was shut. He rapped it gently.

He tried again. He pushed the door open. He moved the curtain and went in.

Something smells wrong! Something has happened

here. The room looked clean. Nothing was awry, nothing spilt or strewn; things were in their usual place: sofa, bed, dressing table, Max Factor lipstick, cosmetics, everything in place. But the phone receiver was hanging off the hook, dangling from its wire hauntingly!

No sign of Anita!

ELEVEN

Ganesh stood in the living room of the empty, silent house and started to think. All of Vasant Vihar echoed the silence. First Sharma. Then Bhaskar. Now Anita?

'No! No! Anita is surely alive. Positively alive. But where? What is the telephone telling me? The one that's dangling off the hook? Where should I start looking for her? She wanted to confess something. What could that be?' Ganesh spoke as he started walking.

He heard a car door slam shut. His palpitations increased. He walked towards the main door.

I should have known better with a girl like you... was the strain of music he heard. Monika followed, twirling the car keys high on her fingers. They managed not to collide. 'Ganesh!' her voice sounded happily startled. 'I was searching for you—I went to your lodgings.'

Ganesh said, 'Monika, Bhaskar is dead.'

'What!' she exclaimed. It was an honestly scared response.

'He was shot dead. Anita is missing.'

'Wait, wait, and take this slowly, Ganesh. What happened?'

Ganesh recounted what had happened. 'I suspected Bhaskar all along. Now he has been eliminated. Anita spoke to me and called me over. I came here. I found no Anita.'

Monika sat facing him. Her eyes shone in fear. She started biting her nails.

'Was the house open?' she asked.

'Yes.'

'Wait. Meenakshi! Meenakshi!' she hollered. Both looked inside expectantly. The clock chimed melodiously. Was it nine o'clock? But no answer…

'Meenakshi must be in the outhouse. Let me go and check.' She started and then stopped midway. 'You come with me too. I am scared.'

'I am not in a mood to see any more bodies.'

'Do you think something may have happened to Anita?'

'I don't have answers to any questions, Monika.'

'Don't shout at me!' she said. 'Ganesh, from this moment on, I shall move in with you. I can't stay in this house. Give me two slices of bread for food. I may need just a bed sheet to sleep. And that will do. I shall move in with you.'

'Let's think of that later. Let's first find Anita.'

'Tonight?'

'Yes.'

Suddenly they thought they heard a loud scream. Monika moved closer. 'Ganesh, please don't leave me alone.'

Meenakshi entered the room, wiping her face with the end of her sari. Seeing Monika and Ganesh standing close to each other, she looked startled.

'Meenakshi, where is Anita?' both asked her.

'Upstairs,' she replied.

'She isn't.'

'Perhaps she has gone out.'

'What kind of a reply is this, Meenakshi? Did you not check where she went?'

'I did not see, Missy.'

'Did you happen to notice where she went last night? Or this morning?'

'I saw her yesterday.'

'Did she go alone?'

'No. She went with Bhaskar Saheb. She must have gone out with him even now.'

They looked at each other. Monika spoke in English to Ganesh, 'I hated Anita, Ganesh. But I never hated her enough to wish her dead.'

Ganesh emphatically replied, 'She isn't dead.' He thought for a while and continued, 'Till now.'

'Meenakshi, wait outside. Where is Ram?'

'Ram may have gone to have some tea.'

'Please wait outside.'

'Has something bad happened, Ganesh Babu?'

'I shall tell you later. Monika, let's inspect Anita's room and your dad's room again. I think the whole mystery is hidden somewhere in your dad's personal life.'

'How do we find Anita?'

'I can't understand head or tail of it.'

'Ganesh, is Bhaskar really dead?'

'I swear he is.'

'How did he die?'

'I'll tell you. First let's take a look at your dad's room. Will you come with me?'

'I certainly shall.' She followed closely behind him, almost as though she was riding piggy-back.

Ganesh could feel her heartbeat on his back. They climbed the stairs together.

Sharma's room was just the same. Nothing had changed after their first visit. Same table, same paper, same photos, newspaper, dust. Nothing out of place.

Ganesh checked the papers one by one. He even painstakingly opened every scrap of paper in the dustbin.

A paper: 'Action, chits, hundis, deposits and savings scheme.'

A letterhead: To Commissioner, Income Tax, Subject: Income tax return for the financial year 1969-70

'Dear Sir...'

A letterhead: Ravi Paper Boards, Avenue Road, Bangalore

Random papers...

Ganesh pulled out the drawers of the table. He shook the alarm clock, lifted the carpet, pushed the chair, and moved the photos on the wall...

He moved to the centre of the room and gazed vacantly all around.

'What are you searching for?'

'I'm not sure.'

He was reading the income tax letter again. 'How did your father amass his wealth, Monika?' he asked.

'He earned it,' she said.

'Brilliant answer! How did he earn it?'

'Through business: export-import of textiles, various

materials. I'm sure there would be some letterhead. Continental Corporation is the name of his company. His office is in Connaught Place.'

'Was he involved in smuggling?'

'Not that I know of. Why do you ask?'

'I'm trying to find reasons for some kind of enmity. I am unable to find anything.'

Ganesh idly opened the newspapers on the table. He kept pushing them around, and then stopped suddenly. One newspaper had caught his interest. The first page had something cut out of it—a portion of a report on the Vietnam war. He noted the date of the paper and pocketed it.

'Do the neighbours buy the Hindustan Times?'

'The neighbour's house is about half a furlong away.'

'Ok, let me go home then,' said Ganesh.

'Me?'

'Would you like to come too?'

'I can't stay alone here. I'll sleep on the floor. But take me with you.'

'I suppose I need to lie on the floor. Do we leave this house unlocked and undisturbed?'

'Meenakshi is there. Ram is there. Whatever happens to this house, I don't really care. The house projects a shadow of death. I don't want to stay here at all. Ganesh, could I be the next in line in the hit list?'

'I don't understand.'

'Dad, Bhaskar, Anita—am I next?'

'Don't be frightened. Come with me.'

As soon as he entered his house, Ganesh went to a neighbour's house and knocked. His neighbour, Rajagopal, was a good and harmless person. He was a quiet man listening to Suprabhatham on the Madras All India Radio on the 60 metres wavelength. Rajagopal opened the door. He was in his vest, with a towel thrown on his shoulder. Right behind him, M. D. Ramanathan was singing Carnatic music in a low bass voice, like out of a cavern.

'Ganesh! How come you are here so late at night? Who is this girl?'

'My client, sir...Sorry, sir...You buy the Hindustan Times, don't you?'

'Yes.'

'I need the paper dated 5th of this month.'

'I heard that there was some fracas in your room last night,' Rajagopal commented as he glared at Monika. He seemed to have developed some dislike for her. A girl with Ganesh, late at night, wearing a man's shirt...

'One of my clients refused to pay me. That's why we got into an argument. I am planning to quit private practice and join some company as a legal adviser. The advertisement was on the 5th paper. I want to give it a shot. Do you have the 5th paper? The Hindustan Times? I buy The Patriot...'

'I shall get it. Viji!' he called his wife.

As soon as Ganesh came back to his room with the paper, he placed it on the table.

Monika was peering over his shoulder. He tried to find the news removed from page 2 of the paper found in Sharma's room.

It was a classified advertisement under 'Real Estate'.

Modern three bedroom bungalow. Shahdara. Plinth area 2400 sq. ft, outer area 4200, new building. Ready for immediate occupation. For sale. Contact Sundar Agencies: 440 816.

Ganesh dialled 440816. It kept ringing for a long time. He put it down in frustration. Monika kept looking at him.

'What advertisement was that?'

'A house ad. A house in Shahdara. Does your dad have any houses in Shahdara?'

'None.'

Ganesh thought for a while. He immediately tried calling Anita's house. *M...m...m...*The hum of an engaged tone...The telephone was still off the hook and dangling. He cursed himself for not having had the sense to place it back.

'There's no one at home!' he said out of context.

'Ganesh, you seem to be worrying too much about Anita,' said Monika.

'Yes, I am worried about what could have happened to her. Are you not worried? However much you hate her, you must realize that basically she is a good woman...'

'I'm actually worried for you.'

Ganesh was silent. What could he do next? *What is the meaning of the classified ad? The same newspaper in Sharma's room had the advertisement removed. A house for sale ad. I must enquire. I shall know only tomorrow. They will have to open the agency. Until then...* he thought.

'We wait...' said Ganesh.

'I feel sleepy, Ganesh.'

'Don't you want to change? Have you eaten?'

'I've had dinner already. I'll just lie down on the ground. Give me a pillow. Even a big book will do.'

'I shall provide you with every comfort. Don't worry.'

'Ganesh, you are an ideal youth. In a similar situation, when a man and a woman are thrown together alone, the man would be tempted and might take advantage of her. He would try something naughty.'

'Monika, in such a bewildering situation, should you even be thinking of such an issue?'

'Ganesh, I am scared. Can't you see how my heart beat has accelerated?'

'It isn't your heart beat, but your youth that is working over-time.'

'Ganesh!' She moved very close to him. He could see her thin lips parting. Her teeth were all regular, except for one. Her teeth actually glowed. She had peppermint breath.

'Ganesh, please save me.'

'How would you like me to?' he asked.

She held on to his arms.

The telephone rang.

It was right next to Monika. She cursed the phone and picked it up. 'Hello!' she said.

'Ganesh! I need Ganesh,' said the voice.

'It's for you,' she said and handed it over to him.

The words were clear. 'Ganesh, you fool, listen. Do you know what happened to Bhaskar? The same fate awaits you. Stop all your monkey business and go back to Madras.'

'Hello! Hello!'

The caller banged down the telephone.

'He hung up!' he said.

'Who was it?' she asked.

'Who?' repeated Ganesh.

'On the phone?'

'Somebody. He advised me to return to Madras.'

'Why?'

'To avoid being killed.'

'A threat?'

'Yes! There seem to be a lot of threats in this case.'

'Ganesh, didn't I pick up the phone first? I have a feeling that I've heard the voice somewhere.'

'Where? Where? Please try to remember. What did he ask you?'

' 'Ganesh! I need Ganesh!' were his words.'

'Whose voice did it resemble?'

'I'm trying to recollect. Hmmmmm...'

Ganesh waited and kept looking at her. She deliberated over the issue. 'Govind?' he suggested.

'I am not able to say for sure. Ganesh, wait!'

He wondered that while he was blindly trusting Monika, was she telling him the entire truth or not? He decided to suspect every one till he learnt the truth.

'Monkey business!'

Where had he heard these familiar words recently?

TWELVE

When Ganesh woke at 7:30 am, he found Monika fast asleep. He pulled a blanket over her and went to make coffee. When he called her, she mumbled something and rolled over. She dozed off again. He again covered her with a blanket and thought of Anita. He thumbed through the pages of the telephone directory.

Flipping through several Sunanda Rays and Sundarrajans , he finally located Sundar Agencies. His finger stopped right there. He noted down the address. He took a bath. He drank black coffee. He bit into a thin slice of bread and thought of Anita again. He glanced through the newspaper. Two more people were murdered in Bengal. 'See you later,' was the message he scribbled for Monika and stepped out.

Ganesh steered through the gentle fog on auto pilot and in a reflective mood. He felt he was growing old. Till now, his profession had not completely stabilized and he had clung on to the momentum of his bravado. He had moved across Bombay, Delhi, Harini, Neeraja, Anita, Monika—the incidents and events had sequentially piled on him. A-ni-ta! Just three syllables, but they carried a haunting, lingering desire in them. Anita. 'Ta': the last syllable meant 'give' in Tamil. So he pondered on what she would give him. He tried calling out her name in various orders: Ani...Anit...Anita...

Anita had hated Sharma. She had hated him for using his huge wealth to buy her and cage her. He had never let her out and had treated her as a vessel of his indulgence, of his pleasure. Could that hate have crystallized sufficiently to make her dare to murder him? Could it have been Anita? A woman who read Omar Khayyam, copied his poetry on a paper and displayed it on her wall. Would she do it? She looked frightened, claimed she needed no property.

Where was Anita?

The agency was in an alley near Golcha Theatre. A man had just opened the agency and was dusting inside. There were a few steel chairs, a steel almirah, a picture of Hanuman (tearing his chest and revealing Lord Rama), and a telephone.

'I am Sundar.' The person who introduced himself was beginning to bald. His moustache sported a lone grey hair. Even his ears sprouted hair. His eyes looked suspicious.

'Namaste! My name is Ganesh. I saw your advertisement. I would like to see the house in Shahdara,' he said.

Sundar's glare seemed to say, 'Your face doesn't look as if you are capable of buying a house.'

'We have sold the Shahdara house,' he said.

'Is that so? For how much?'

'I don't have to reveal that.'

Ganesh glanced around. 'Mr. Sundar, can we talk alone?'

Sundar's eyes reflected more suspicion and caution. 'What do you want to talk?'

'This is the matter. I...I mean my client...You see, I am a lawyer. In the industrial area of Shahdara, my client has a PVC factory. So he badly needs a house in that area. In case the house that you advertised has not been sold, he would even pay some extra—say seventy-five to hundred more. I can pay you a hefty commission too.'

Sundar's face brightened with the word 'commission'. 'Be seated. Would you like to have tea?'

'No, thank you. What about the house?'

'Who is your client?' asked Sundar.

'Shah, a Gujarati.'

'But...the house is sold.'

'Who bought it?' asked Ganesh.

'Someone called Sharma.'

'R. K. Sharma?'

'Yes.'

'I know him. Did he come in person?'

'No. His secretary handled the whole deal. His name is Bhaskar. They have signed the sale deed, paid the advance. There are some papers pending verification. Ninety per cent payment is done. Bhaskar may come today. You can probably meet him.'

'Bhaskar isn't in a position to come here,' said Ganesh.

'You know Bhaskar too?'

'I know him fairly well. I shall talk to them. When did they buy the house?'

'They came here the day after the ad was released and completed the deal. They were in such a rush that they immediately accepted the stated price.'

'Where is the house?'

'In Shahdara.'

'I am sure it's staying put in Shahdara. It can't move. But where in Shahdara?'

'You know the industrial area, right? You need to go past that on the main road, towards north; a furlong down and you will find a theatre. I think it's Apsara. You need to go past that, turn left and go for a mile...it's an isolated bungalow named "Yamuna", with empty plots on either side. The whole area has just about two or three houses. It isn't yet developed.'

'Thank you, Mr. Sundar. I shall call on them.'

Ganesh decided go to Shahdara directly. But once he crossed Red Fort, he had a change of heart. He visited Inspector Rajesh, but he wasn't available. He decided to visit another officer that Rajesh had recommended. Luckily, he was available.

'I need the late R. K. Sharma's post mortem report, please.'

'Are you the lawyer?'

'Yes. I take care of his estate and business. I need to see the report.'

'It will be tough for me to give you the report.'

'Why?'

'Are you serious? It's tough to part with police records.'

'I just need to see it. That's all.'

'Would you please get a letter of permission from the ASP?'

'Where is the ASP's room?'

'You need to go to Tilak Marg. His office isn't here.'

'Oh my God!'
'Sorry! I can't do much.'
'Inspector Rajesh said...'
'Rajesh doesn't know the rules.'

Ganesh came out of the police station very disappointed. A man approached him. He asked Ganesh, 'Sir, what do you want?'

'I need to see a post mortem report, that's it. By the way, who are you?'

'Which case?'

'Sharma: R. K. Sharma. The post mortem was done last month.'

'Please come away from here. You should not approach the inspector for all this. Don't you know that there are many clerks around?'

Long live corruption! thought Ganesh.

At first, the report disappointed him. It didn't have any of the desired elements he expected. Sharma's identity, cause of death: all were in long, convoluted Latin terms. He flipped through the file slowly: government papers, hand-written testimonies, signatures and witnesses.

Ganesh stared at the file for some time. He frowned, sighed and left.

He went to a PCO and called Inspector Rajesh again. The inspector answered the call.

'Ganesh here. I am going from Delhi to Shahdara today. I should be back in the evening. I thought of keeping you posted.'

'Why Shahdara?'

'Sharma's case. I am going there based on a hunch.'

'Have you discovered anything?'

'It's still a puzzle. The puzzle deepens and is complex. But by this evening I shall know one way or the other.'

'You seem to be quite sure...'

'No! A small tweet of instinct that it could end this evening...I need your permission to leave. Since Bhaskar is dead, I don't want you to think that I am on the run.'

'Ok! Get back soon. Bhaskar's body has been sent for autopsy.'

Ganesh crossed the river Yamuna and sped on the asphalt. Uttar Pradesh government buses hurtled past him like blue demons. Indira Gandhi was smiling from all the trees. Passing jeeps carried the Jan Sangh's yellow flags. The flags were fluttering and seeking votes.

As soon as he reached Shahdara town, he was welcomed by yellow walls. Family planning advertisements were painted on the walls—inverted triangles followed by some smiling faces. Right next to them were ads for fertility specialists promising to cure erectile dysfunctions. The loudspeakers were blasting songs from *Aradhana*. But Ganesh's car speed actually distorted the songs with a Doppler effect and the pitch changed. Turbanned farmers crossed the road with no care for the cars. A bull stood its ground like it was the chief minister. On the dusty roads, plenty of children chased Ambassador cars carrying speakers blaring election campaign slogans.

Ganesh stopped his car in an Esso petrol bunk. He parked it there and told the staff that he would collect it in a short while. He started walking. He looked out for Apsara theatre and found it. He walked past it and turned left. He proceeded further. He spotted sugarcane fields. Soon after, he saw some empty plots. There were white stones marking plots.

There was just one house which seemed to have magically appeared on the horizon, obstructing the emptiness. It had sprung up suddenly as though out of Aladdin's lamp. Distempered in a bright colour, it gleamed resplendently.

A big bungalow.

It had a small iron gate. He opened it noiselessly. It was a killer silence. No trees, no twitter of birds, no shade; the silence of the deserts prevailed. Ganesh walked stealthily towards the shade of the porch. Even his footsteps could be heard distinctly. What a long walk!

He reached the porch. The main door was shut, but didn't appear locked. The wall had a bright white switch with the imprint of a small red bell. Ganesh's finger was about to ring the bell. He withdrew at the last moment. He scanned the building. The garage was locked. Was there a car inside? All the windows were shut. He walked around the house slowly. He avoided the concrete paving and walked on the grass. His actions indicated that he was investigating the house knowing full well that what he was doing was illegal. But his enthusiasm propelled him. When he crept around the corner, he hesitated and looked around, then continued. Edged around the compound wall were plenty of flower pots with withered plants.

It was mid-afternoon. Short shadows; with no breeze, it was a stifling atmosphere.

Ganesh felt spooked and his hands were clammy. It seemed like he expected something to happen. But what?

On the third side of the house, a window was open. Ganesh's heart missed a beat. Someone was definitely inside. He peeked in cautiously. Slowly...D-e-a-d slow!

He could see a kitchen. A gas stove. A few vessels. A refrigerator. It was open. A few Coke bottles were stacked in it. She picked up one.

Anita!

Ganesh hid immediately. Anita could not have noticed him.

She is here! Thankfully alive! And so am I, finally alive! he thought joyfully.

Ganesh thought mometarily of running to the front of the door and banging on the door, but waited, planning to observe some more.

He remained plastered to the wall.

The Coke was opened. The sound of the lid being prised open. The sound of the liquid gurgling into a glass when poured.

Silence again. Underlying silence. Then a deep male voice was heard.

'Anita!'

Silence.

'Anita!'

'Mm...'

'Come here!' not a plain invitation but a lusty come-hither.

Silence again.

'Anita, can't you hear me?'

Ganesh thought: *Where have I heard this voice? Where, oh, where?*

'Anita!'

He could hear it close by. The person must have entered the kitchen.

That voice! Yes! The very same voice. The one that had warned him yesterday on the phone. The one that warned that Bhaskar's fate awaited him. Yes!

Should he peek in? No.

'Leave me alone! Please! Please! I beg of you! Just leave me!'

Anita's bangles were rattling. Ganesh's blood stirred in anger. Who was he?

'Just once, Anita! Just this once!'

'Please! Please!'

The glass fell and broke. He could hear the glass splinter.

The voices faded and moved out of the room. Ganesh decided not to delay any further. He rushed towards the front door to kick it open and save Anita. When he crossed the window, he happened to peer through it.

The kitchen was empty. But there was a mirrored wardrobe next to the kitchen. He could see their images reflected in the mirror. They were in the next room. Anita and the person to whom the voice belonged...

Anita was seated on the bed, head bent down. The man facing her was gesticulating heavily and talking intently. His identity stunned Ganesh out of his wits.

Ganesh ignored everything, everyone; he left the house and ran towards his car.

THIRTEEN

Ganesh kept running. He realized that speed was paramount. He could think of nothing but the rush. He reached the main road and was crossing the Shahdara telephone exchange. He paused. He panted. In front of the exchange was a PCO booth. He reached it, searched for change, dialled and said, 'Hello!'

(*At times, I'm just a fool. I should have guessed this long back. Tch!* he thought, as he mentally kicked himself.)

'Rajesh speaking.'

'This is Ganesh here. A very significant matter has cropped up in Sharma's case. Can you immediately come to Shahdara in your jeep?'

'What is it?'

'The case is solved. It's done, Inspector Saheb.'

'Which case? Sharma's or Bhaskar's? We have two murders on hand.'

'Both.'

'Have you found Govind?'

'I have information about him. Please come right away. Bring four or five of your men. It's all over. It's too complicated to be explained over the phone. Another thing—could you please go to my house and pick up Sharma's daughter Monika on your way? She's waiting for me there. I'll call her and keep her informed. Please come soon. Do you know my address?'

'Yes. We got it written down yesterday. Ganesh, can't you give some details? I am not able to follow anything.'

'I am not bluffing. I shall explain right from the start. No worries. But right now, I don't have time for details.'

'Where in Shahdara?'

'On the main road is Apsara theatre. Take a left turn adjacent to that. You will cross a sugar cane field and some empty plots. Right in the middle of that emptiness is a brand new bungalow. You can't miss it. But you must come immediately.' He hung up.

He searched in his pocket for more change. He was running short of change. He walked to a shop nearby, got some change and dialled his home number.

'Monika! Are you up and about?'

'Ganesh! Where are you?'

'Shahdara.'

'Where the hell is Shahdara?'

'Let me tell you. No! Listen, in a short while from now, Inspector Rajesh will come over. You accompany him. I am waiting for you here. You must certainly come.'

'What happened?'

'Your dad's case is resolved.'

'Have you found out who the murderer is?'

'Why don't you come and see for yourself?'

'Ganesh! Is it Anita?'

'Not at all!'

'Then who?'

'Can't tell you over the phone. You must come. It's important that you come. Do you understand? Your presence is mandatory. You are needed. I don't have time now. I'm sorry.' He hung the receiver on its hook.

Due to some error, the telephone spat out twenty paisa. He thought it was his lucky day.

Ganesh walked around. An election booth faced him. Small children were singing anti-Indira songs in silly rhymes.

The loudspeaker asked in an intimidating tone: 'What is socialism?' A cow turned around, suspicious of socialism.

Ganesh thought over. Made, a decision. He went into the shop and purchased a clipped pad, pencil ('Please sharpen it for me') and some white sheets. He approached the election booth. The party members were distributing badges with the picture of a lamp. He collected one and pinned it on his chest.

He rushed back to the house. It took him ten long minutes to reach the isolated bungalow. He opened the gate. Unlike the first time, he did not bother with caution or silence. He strode in purposefully and rang the bell. The locked door had a magic eye. Through it, people inside could check who was outside. Ganesh turned his back to it.

Some time passed. He rang the bell again.

Some more time elapsed. The door opened a crack. 'Who is it?' Anita's voice. It opened fractionally. He could see Anita; she was dishevelled.

Ganesh put his finger on his lips and warned her. 'Silence!' he shushed her. Anita's eyes had a startling array of emotions: surprise, fear, terror, a ray of happiness.

She gestured to him to go away.

He gestured why.

She held her fingers like a pistol and shot him silently at his chest, indicating that his life was in danger.

Ganesh used both his hands to form two pistols and shot them exuberantly and said, 'Don't fear.'

Facing him were thick curtains; behind her a male voice asked: 'Who is it?'

Ganesh recognized that voice, and said: 'Elections, sir. I have come to canvass. Asking for your vote.'

'Go away,' Anita kept gesturing.

'Tell him that none of us have voting power here.'

'I am trying to tell...'

'Sorry, sir. The list carries two votes here. Mr. Madanagopal and Mrs. Sushma Yadav. Are you Mrs. Yadav?'

Anita begged and shook her head. 'Please!' she implored and beseeched him to leave.

'There is no such person here. Wrong address. Ask him to leave,' commanded the voice.

But the voice was careful not to step out from behind the curtain.

'No, sir. The address is right. Sir, could you please come out?'

'Anita, ask him to leave!'

'He refuses to!'

'Tell him we will throw him out! We will collar him.'

'Sir, please don't say that! After all I have come here seeking votes. That's all. Can I come in?'

'No!' said the screen.

'I am coming in!'

'Tell him that his bones will crack if he steps in. No vote, nothing. Ask him to stand outside the door. We are new here. We don't have any vote here.'

'Are you not Mr. Yadav?'

'Get out!'

'Could you please come out? Why are you so harsh?'

'Please, don't come in! Danger!' signed Anita.

'Wait,' he signed to Anita.

'Is he leaving or not?'

'No sir!'

'I'll teach him a lesson.'

The screen rustled. The man was visible. Thin lips, bushy eyebrows, broad forehead and the stubble of a few days, paired with cruel eyes.

'Pleased to meet you, sir. Indira's government is criticizing the ruling government's grant and subsidy. And they want to remove it. But do they even realize the value of it? It's just about Hindustan Steel's loss of one quarter...'

'Get lost.'

'Why, sir? Are you a supporter of the Congress?'

'Congress M! M for murder.'

'Will you please get me a glass of water? Who is this girl? Is she your daughter?' asked Ganesh.

'Do you know what I have in my hand?'

'Is it a pistol?'

'Please don't. Please, I'm scared,' said Anita.

'Anita, come in,' said the man.

Anita was stunned.

'This is a real gun. Go away!'

'What is my crime? I am asking for votes on behalf of Jan Sangh? Is that a crime? Why are you pointing your gun at me?'

'Bahadur! Where did he vanish?'

'Who is Bahadur? Your bodyguard, huh?'

'Hey! Get out!' said the man.

'Mr. Yadav!'

'I am not Yadav!'

Ganesh gave him a powerful kick. The gun fell out of his hands and flew near Anita.

'I have not come seeking votes. My name is Ganesh.' He kept eyeing the gun that had fallen on the floor. The man's expression changed.

'Ganesh! You have come here too? Bahadur! Bahadur!' the man started walking towards the gun.

'Don't move! If you do…' said Ganesh. 'Anita, pick up that gun. Don't fear.'

'Anita, does he know who I am?' asked the man.

'Have you told him?'

'No,' she shook her head.

'Anita! Pick up that gun,' said Ganesh.

'Pick that gun and give it to me, Anita,' said the man.

'Why? Do you need to kill again? I know you very well. I also know who you are.'

The man pounced on Ganesh. But Ganesh was younger. The other man pounced without any dexterity, a blind move. Ganesh used the speed of the opponent to trip him. The man hit a chair and fell down. He stood up, his anger increased.

Anita: A Trophy Wife / 131

'Anita, give me the gun!' he demanded. 'Anita! Don't give!' instructed Ganesh.

Anita had picked up the gun. She was holding it in her hands.

'Anita! Shoot him! Shoot!'

Anita grabbed it tight in both hands and said, 'Ganesh!' She aimed at him.

'Anita, would you shoot me?'

'Shoot, Anita, go on!'

'Anita! Cast it away! Throw it out of the window!'

'No, don't throw!'

Anita backed up. She opened the window. The man ran towards her. Ganesh held on to him tight.

'Leave me. You don't seem to know me. After having met me here, you cannot leave this house alive. I must kill you and bury you!'

'Don't move! Anita...hmmmm.'

Anita threw the gun out of the window. The man's strength seemed to vanish at that gesture. He tried to vent his anger on Ganesh, but couldn't. Ganesh pushed him up against the wall and punched him. 'Does it hurt?' he asked. He landed a professional upper cut. 'Does it hurt?' He could see a trickle of blood in the man's jaw.

Anita kept looking unblinkingly.

'Anita! What shall I do?' asked Ganesh.

'Kill him,' she said. 'Take your time and kill him deliberately.'

'Bahadur!' the man yelled at the top of his voice. The nerves in his throat had worked up to a huge scream.

Footsteps were heard. Someone came running.

Bahadur, who entered the room, was tall and gigantic. He was wearing a khaki shirt. He had tiny eyes, a moustache, and seemed to have muscles like a model for a bullworker advertisement.

'Anita, get into the other room. Lock yourself in! Quick...' screamed Ganesh.

Bahadur-Ganesh.

Ganesh-Bahadur.

Bahadur approached Ganesh. Anita was temporarily safe. The gun was lying outside!

Ganesh got anxious.

'When the opponent is stronger and you are unarmed, to defeat him there are only two options—one, hit him below the belt; two, focus all his strength, divert it and make him fall down.' Ganesh recollected his judo lessons.

Bahadur approached cautiously. Ganesh targeted his hip and kicked with all his might.

Bahadur stepped away and laughed. A humourless laugh. He knew the art!

Bahadur's left arm moved in a half-circle and a flash landed on Ganesh's jaw.

When the man saw Ganesh falling down, he instructed coldly: 'Give him one on his belly. Hold him. Let me have the honour.'

Bahadur was distracted for a moment. That was enough. Just that moment to raise his knee and jam it into Bahadur's lower abdomen. For the first time Bahadur must have felt pain. He pounced on Ganesh with all his pent-up anger. Ganesh recovered quickly and moved. Bahadur fell on the door; the door swung open and slammed shut. Ganesh pinned Bahadur down. The man now leapt on top of Ganesh. Bahadur got up with plenty of stamina left. Again, both Bahadur and the man pounded Ganesh.

Ganesh felt that every inch of his body had broken and crumbled into pieces. He fell on the ground helplessly.

'Bahadur! There's a gun outside the window. Fetch it,' said the man.

He looked at Ganesh and said, 'Where do I shoot you? On your forehead or your belly?'

FOURTEEN

Ganesh looked directly into the man's eyes.

'What do you gain by killing me?' he asked.

'You shouldn't have seen me!'

'Even before what I saw registers in my mind, if you—' Ganesh started.

'Don't talk, Ganesh! Bahadur! Did you get the gun?' shouted the man.

No reply. Ganesh remarked, 'That calendar looks good.'

'Do you want to impress on me that you are indifferent to your death? Why don't you tell me if the calendar looks good after the lead of the bullet hits your bloodstream?'

'Lead?'

'Yes...Bahadur!'

'Ji Saheb!' his voice was heard outside the window.

'Did you get it?'

'The grass is over grown and wild...Saheb! Look there!'

'What?'

'A jeep is approaching! I think it is a police jeep.'

He went to the window and peered out. 'Bahadur! *Jaldi*! Go to the garage! Start the car!' He turned to Ganesh.

The cruelty in his eyes sent panic waves into Ganesh.

'It could be an election jeep,' said Ganesh.

'Bastard! You...you...' he came closer.

'Easy sir, easy! It may take some time for you to kill

me with your bare hands.' Ganesh curled himself into a foetal position.

He could hear rolling shutters being opened outside. A car door being slammed; it sputtered in a rush, then started, vroomed and came very near.

'Saheb! Come quickly!'

The man's punch landed half-heartedly on Ganesh's shoulder.

'Mmm! Slowly, take your time. Hit me. No rush.'

He kicked Ganesh with his boot, but Ganesh grabbed it. The car horn was heard. 'Saheb!'

The man shook his leg free. He went near the window again and peeked out. 'Hey! I shall not forget you. I shall not forget till I kill you!' he said.

'What's the hurry, sir?'

He ran. He ran with just one boot. Ganesh could move only with great effort. He limped to the window.

A jeep was coming on the mud road in a huge cloud of dust. A black Ambassador left the house at the same time on a rutted road. The car avoided the jeep, turned into a fork of the road and disappeared.

The jeep stopped. Seemed to think for awhile...

'Chase it! Chase it!' Ganesh screamed his heart off to the jeep. They couldn't possibly hear him.

The Ambassador bumped down the rut road in a dust cloud, like a car in a stunt movie, and reached the main road. Meanwhile, the hesitant jeep approached Ganesh.

Ganesh was frustrated. He noticed that the Ambassador was moving north on the main road.

The jeep halted in front of the house. Monika jumped out and looked around searchingly.

'I'm here!' said Ganesh.

She smiled at him. Inspector Rajesh and three constables alighted.

'Please come quickly!' screamed Ganesh.

Monika entered the house. 'My God! What happened, Ganesh? Why is there so much blood on you?'

'Had a fight. They hit me and escaped. Rajesh! Quick... Follow that Ambassador.'

'Who is in it?'

'The culprit.'

'Who?'

'I shall tell you.'

'There's another jeep reaching here.'

'Don't waste time. Follow right away. The car went north on the main road.'

Rajesh ran out.

'Where is Anita?' asked Monika.

'She has locked herself up in the other room.' They could hear the jeep start. Rajesh came in.

'Are you not going with them?' asked Ganesh.

'Another jeep will arrive shortly. Let's all go in that. We have a radio in it. We can inform the control room through that. We can go to Meerut...We shall nab them. What is the car number?'

Ganesh knocked the door, 'Anita! Anita! Do you hear me? Anita! It's me, Ganesh. They have left. It's just the three of us—Inspector Rajesh Monika and I. Open the door.'

A soft voice was heard: 'Why is the inspector here? Is it to arrest me?'

'No,' reassured Ganesh.

'What's happening? I don't understand,' said Rajesh.

'I shall explain on the way...Anita! Nothing shall happen to you. I stand guarantee- I am a lawyer.'

'Ganesh, will you protect me?'

'Till the end, Anita!'

The door opened. Anita stood there. She looked as nervous as a cornered rat who had stepped out of a trap... well...not a rat. Maybe a rabbit, a deer...oh Man! Oh man! No time to imagine her eyes and make comparisons...

'Anita!' called out Monika.

'Moni! Do you know?'

'No, Anita! What is it?'

'I shall explain everything. Anita, be quiet for some time. Inspector Rajesh, you can take Anita's statement later,' said Ganesh masterfully.

'I am unable to comprehend anything, Ganesh!'

'I shall let you into it, Inspector! But right now, our top priority would be to nab the car.'

'We shall surely nab them.'

The second jeep honked outside.

'Let's go!' shouted Ganesh. 'Anita! Monika! Both of you come!' He ran out.

They followed him.

'Welcome to Meerut,' said the signboard.

A short distance away was a check post to stop traffic.

The black and yellow painted crane of the barricade was fully raised.

A temporary shack had a table, a chair, a bench, a mud pot for water, a glass on top of it; two lazy people sprawled on the bench. The shack was for collecting the Octroi. A few trucks were parked, awaiting their turn.

Some Sardarjis were sipping tea from tall glasses in a nearby tea shop. The man on the chair, an accountant, made another error in computing the amount in the receipt. A town jeep stopped and policemen jumped out of it. Two of them approached the accountant and one of the lazy men brought the barricade down. Another fellow took a red flag and held it in front with a warning sign board to stop.

The constable lit a cigarette.

'Stop the Ambassador car, black, TLK 1836 or 1386, when it comes to the check post. Others can be allowed to pass...OK?' he instructed the check post operator.

The other policeman nodded his head in agreement and borrowed a match.

(Right at that moment, Bahadur looked into the rear-view mirror.)

'Sir! I see a jeep! They are following us.'

The man looked around. 'Step on it! Step on the accelerator.'

The needle crossed a 100.

Meanwhile, at the Meerut check post, the constable said, 'I shall wait on the other side.'

'Hold the post low!'

'Shall I tie it down, Sahib?'

'Don't tie it! Hold on to it. Let the buses and lorries go. Only detain the car.'

(The ambassador's needle danced between 100 and 110.)

'Did you watch *'Tum haseen main jawaan*?' asked the constable.

'No,' responded the other.

'Hema Malini and Dharmendar...*Accha* picture.'

('Idiot! Step on it Bahadur!'

'Sahib! The accelerator is touching the floor.')

'Welcome to Meerut!' read the board. A short distance away was the check post...

'Look out, Bahadur...'

It was too late.

The barricade crashed on the windshield. The glass broke into splinters, and the cracks spread across like webs.

Bahadur lost control of the vehicle at the speed of 110 km per hour.

The Ambassador moved away from the road, rose on two of its wheels, sped for two seconds, banged into a tree and turned turtle. Its entire chassis was visible and the rear wheels were still spinning...The horn had jammed and was blowing loudly.

Sardarjis, the lazy man sprawled in the shack, two constables...all ran to the car.

'What happened?' asked Rajesh.

'Sir, we got a message from Delhi to stop the black

Ambassador. We enforced a road block. The car crashed recklessly.'

'What happened to the people inside?' asked Ganesh.

'The driver is alive, but unconscious. The other man seated in the front is dead. He had no chance of survival.'

'Monika!' called Ganesh. Monika stepped out of the jeep. 'Anita, stay here. Rajesh, please come with me.' Ganesh explained: 'Monika, what you are going to see now will be shocking. I regret that I need to make you see this. But it is imperative that you do. Please pardon me, Monika. Please come along, Rajesh.'

Anita sat in the jeep with her head bent down. The other three went to the car lying bottom-up. An ambulance was waiting at a distance. A stretcher had been placed near the car. Two white uniformed staff placed the body gently on the stretcher.

'Monika, go near and see.'

Monika approached closer. She let out such a loud piercing scream in such loud decibels that the birds were scared out of the trees and flew away.

'Dad! My dad!' she kept screaming.

'How is it possible? Ganesh! My God! I can't believe this!' said Rajesh.

They returned to the jeep. Monika was completely devastated. Her clothes and hair were in a state. She had a vacant stare and continued to sob with every kilometre passed.

'I need aspirin,' said Anita.

'I shall ask the driver to stop when we reach a medical shop. Rajesh, what did you say?'

'It's unbelievable.'

'Anita, tell us.'

'Ganesh, will I be sent to prison?'

'Why?'

'For having spoken a lie.'

'Why don't you explain the circumstances that forced you to lie? Inspector, don't take any notes now. Please pay attention.'

'Anita, your husband was one jealous man. Right?'

'Yes.'

'He completely possessed you, and claimed that as a right; isn't that true?'

'Yes, he made me a total slave.'

'So you were gripped by an all-consuming hatred for him?'

'True.'

'What were his feelings for you?'

'Lust. Envy. More lust. More envy.'

'What sort of a person was Govind?'

'A silent man. Humble. Deep. He used to make my bed. He used to even lay out my sandals. He would only look at my feet. But...'

'But?'

'Just once, in my room, he...me...'

'Did you inform your husband of it?'

'No. He saw it himself.'

'What did he do?'

'Sharma used a whip. He ruthlessly whipped Govind, who fainted. He gave Govind water and revived him. Then he whipped Govind again right in front of my eyes! It was supposed to be a lesson for me!'

'What happened to Govind?'

'He died.'

'What did your husband do?'

'He panicked. He did not expect that. He called Bhaskar.'

'What did Bhaskar do?'

'He thought over it. He spoke to my husband. He asked for my husband's shirt, his shoes, his wallet, his visiting card and the keys for the small car. He dragged Govind on the floor...'

'What did your husband instruct you to do after that?'

'He instructed: 'Govind's body will be discovered in Ridge Road after some time. The police will call you. They will want you to identify the body. You should make a positive identification that it is my body.' He wanted the police to believe that the dead man was Sharma and that Govind was absconding.'

'Why did you agree?'

'Deliberately. He had total control over me for years. He practically lorded over me. This was my chance to rule over him. For many days he had kept me in a cage, huh? This seemed like a golden opportunity for me to keep him in hiding under lock and key and not even let a ray of sunlight in. His life hinged on my words!'

'What sort of a person was Bhaskar?'

'An opportunist...As soon as I identified Govind's body as my husband's, he took care of all the other arrangements. Soon after the post mortem, he took urgent steps to cremate the body.'

'Monika received the news of her father's death late. Was this delay deliberate?'

'Yes.'

'The reason? That Monika shouldn't spill the beans about the dead man's identity. No one should identify the dead man as anybody other than Mr. Sharma.'

'Yes.'

'Where was Sharma?'

'He went into hiding at the Shahdara house. An independent bungalow that he bought in a rush.'

'Then he never came out of the Shahdara house?'

'He came out just once.'

'Why?'

'To kill Bhaskar,' said Anita. Deadly silence prevailed in the jeep.

'Bhaskar had gained courage. He was having this bravado because he knew Sharma's life was in his hands. He started to blackmail Sharma, and asked for a lot of money. He also showed undue interest in me...tried to play around with me. I have already told you of this, Ganesh!'

'Who killed Bhaskar...?'

'Sharma! Bhaskar failed to realize one thing. The trap that he laid would entrap him. Sharma shot Bhaskar dead.'

'Then?'

'I received your telephone call that night. By the time I tried to escape, my husband arrived. He abducted me under gun point to the Shahdara house. He kept me there with him. Three days, Ganesh! Three solid days of torture! Sharma should not have died in this car accident so quickly.'

She continued, 'Monika! I am tired of being beautiful. I am tired of rolling in money. The cheap comforts of this life are enough. Enough of being stripped of my clothes at gun point...Monika! You please live in that monster's gilded mansion! I don't need anything...not even a penny from it! I have no one in my life! No one!'

'Anita, I am there for you,' said Ganesh.

'Ganesh!' said Monika.

BEFORE WE FINISH...

His name is Anand. Her name is Radhika. He took her along.

An oversized concrete wall...Behind that were a pool and an artificial waterfall...

'Anand, why should we hide and duck and find this place of isolation? We are married, right?'

'Baby, you just wouldn't understand. There's a thrill,' said Anand.